A Scream in Soho

A Scream in Soho

John G. Brandon

With an Introduction
by Martin Edwards

Poisoned Pen Press

Originally published in London in 1940 by Wright & Brown
Copyright © 2014 The British Library
Introduction Copyright © 2014 Martin Edwards

Published by Poisoned Pen Press in association with the
British Library

First Edition 2016
First US Trade Paperback Edition

10 9 8 7 6 5 4 3 2 1

Library of Congress Catalog Card Number: 2016933722

ISBN: 9781464206498   Trade Paperback

Poisoned Pen Press
6962 E. First Ave., Ste. 103
Scottsdale, AZ 85251
www.poisonedpenpress.com
info@poisonedpenpress.com

Printed in the United States of America

Contents

Introduction

A Scream in Soho is an appealing title for a lively, lurid thriller set in London during the early days of the Second World War. The hero is Inspector Patrick Aloysius McCarthy of Scotland Yard, a handsome extrovert with an intimate knowledge of his native Soho, and a love of the area not lessened by his awareness of its dark side.

The darkness takes a literal form as the story opens, for it is night-time, during a black-out. Laws introduced on the eve of war demanded that windows and doors should be covered, so as to prevent the escape of any glimmer of light that might assist enemy aircraft. This created conditions ideally suited to crime, and in real life, a sociopath called Gordon Frederick Cummins exploited the black-out to murder four women and attempt to kill two more. Two years before Cummins wrote himself into history as "the Black-Out Ripper," John G. Brandon captures the surreal atmosphere of gloomy "phoney war" London, and above all of sleazy yet strangely exciting Soho.

Brandon offers a vivid picture of the cosmopolitan mix of people who inhabit the labyrinth of streets in the *demi-monde*. As well as Italians like the cafe owner Lucia Spadoglia, the population includes not only Austrian and German refugees, "harmless people who had suffered miseries almost beyond belief," but also gangsters such as Floriello Mascagni, who hang around race-tracks by day and haunt the clubs and dance-halls by night. Against this background, Assistant Commissioner Haynes's claim that crimes of violence have "dropped to practically nothing" is a hostage to fortune. An hour or so after he utters those words, a scream is heard in Soho Square, but when the police go to investigate, they find a three-edged stiletto and a woman's handkerchief, both covered in blood—but no sign of a murder victim. Before long, however, a corpse is discovered, and after that the body count rises relentlessly.

Brandon's pacy narrative is packed with melodrama and colourful characters. As well as that vanishing victim, we encounter a transvestite Prussian, a pickpocket working for the police, stolen papers likely to help the Nazis to win the war, a glamorous baroness with something to hide—and a sinister dwarf called Ludwig. At least McCarthy, an affable maverick, keeps his head while all around are losing theirs, even when his adversary gives "a low, animal-like growl" before hissing, "Curse you. Whatever happens, you at least, will not be there to see it!"

This is a period piece not just in its depiction of London during the "phoney war" but also in literary terms. Brandon was not aiming to create an elaborate whodunnit of the kind for which Agatha Christie and Dorothy L. Sayers became famous, but rather a thriller to rank alongside the work of Edgar Wallace (who had died eight years earlier), Sax Rohmer, Sapper and Sydney Horler. He was writing at a time when there was a sharp divide between the two styles of popular fiction. Sayers was prominent in the Detection Club, which excluded thriller writers from membership, and aimed for literary excellence. Edgar Wallace and his disciples produced large quantities of cheerfully low-brow entertainment quite lacking in pretension and pomposity, and displaying social attitudes that are bound to make modern readers wince. Yet Soho attracted Sayers and her colleagues just as much as it did Brandon. The Detection Club had its meeting rooms in Gerrard Street, a stone's throw from McCarthy's home in Dean Street, and once famous for the "43", run by the legendary Queen of the Night-Clubs, Kate Meyrick.

A Scream in Soho ranks as one of the best among dozens of books written by John Gordon Brandon, but information about him is now almost as hard to come by as copies of his books, and bibliographic confusion is exacerbated by the fact that his son, Gordon Brandon, also wrote crime fiction. Born in Australia in 1879, Brandon senior became a professional heavy-weight boxer before moving to Britain after the First World War. He became a prolific contributor to magazines such as *The Thriller*, and was one of many authors to write instalments in the long-running Sexton Blake series, creating Blake's monocled, drawling associate "R.S.V.P.". His full-length debut, *The Big Heart*, published in 1923, showed the influence of Sapper's stories about Bulldog Drummond.

Sayers and Christie started their careers as novelists at roughly the same time as Brandon. Sayers actually dabbled in writing about Sexton Blake herself before settling down to life with Lord Peter Wimsey, while Christie's second book, *The Secret Adversary*, was a breezy thriller not very different from Brandon's novels. But Sayers and Christie soon focused their energies on howdunnits and whodunnits, while Brandon remained focused on thrillers catering for the mass market. Books like *Death Tolls the Gong* and *The Yellow Mask* owed a debt to Rohmer, creator of Fu Manchu, and he co-wrote a play, *The Silent House*, which again featured enigmatic Chinese characters. Brandon also rewrote several Sexton Blake storylines for novels that he published outside that franchise. These offered a slightly modified version of R.S.V.P. called the Honourable Arthur Stukely Pennington, who is assisted by a valet known as Flash George Wibley, "the ace of high-class cracksmen." Brandon's work gives a flavour of its time, and the way he captures a remarkable phase in London's history makes *A Scream in Soho* intriguing in ways even such an imaginative man would scarcely have contemplated.

Martin Edwards

Chapter I

A Stranger in Soho

In that inexpressibly comfortable little Soho café, owned and managed by that dignified Italian lady, the Signora Lucia Spadoglia, Inspector McCarthy sat and waited.

A neighbouring clock had just chimed out the hour of eleven upon a night which might easily have given birth to Henley's immortal line "black as the pit from pole to pole," for in the considered opinion of the inspector—not to mention a few million other human gropers at that moment in the metropolis and its environs—it was all that, and blacker.

Outside the cheerful walls of the signora's oasis the blackout was in full blast, and whatever helpful gleam of light there might have come from the skies in the broader main thoroughfares, the narrow, built-in streets of dingy Soho got none of it. In that truly cosmopolitan area it was, to use the truly expressive term of the good Father O'Hara, creeping about upon his nightly round of visits to the sick and ailing, as "black as the hobs of hell!"

Inspector McCarthy had had what he considered to be his fair share of it that night. For the past three hours, and by the doubtful aid of a dimmed torch, he had been paying visits to those cheaper cafés, and in particular *delicatessen* shops, in the Charing Cross Road and adjacent thoroughfares, which the Austrian and German refugees were wont to patronize. Harmless people who had suffered miseries almost beyond belief for the greater part, and who were filled with nothing but an immense and overflowing gratitude towards the land which had given them shelter in their hour of direst need. Still objects of pity to the soft-hearted McCarthy, notwithstanding the obvious improvement in their condition since arrival here.

But—and it was a very large "but"—there were others; those ugly little black sheep who creep into every flock and, indeed, are there only for their own ulterior purposes. Gentry, and, sad to say, ladies, who could do incalculable harm if their activities were not speedily checked. Hence the number of Special-Branch operators, expert linguists, he had observed mingling unostentatiously among the patrons of such places.

It was with almost the ecstasy of a devout Moslem gazing for the first time upon the walls of Mecca that he had fumbled his way into the well-blacked-out doorway of Signora Spadoglia's premises and blinked at its well-lit warmth and comfort, generally.

The signora, as has been written elsewhere, was a protégée of Inspector McCarthy. Time was when the premises were occupied as a pin-table saloon, the rendezvous of as tough a gang of thugs as Soho could show. It was run then by certain Semitic gentry—who combined business in nearby Berwick Street, with horse-racing and, additionally, Detective-Inspector McCarthy proved later, a side line in certain well-camouflaged and extremely payable "fencing" activities.

The inspector having piloted these gentry successfully, first through the Marlborough Street seat of Justice, and then the Old Bailey to durance vile, the place closed down and for a long time it was the home of nothing but cobwebs. Which, as it stood upon the corner of two busy streets and was unquestionably an excellent business stand, seemed a pity.

It was after it had remained in this condition for several months that the Signora Spadoglia, whose evening cooking of spaghetti, macaroni and other cereal edibles beloved of the Italian palate was famed from Soho to Clerkenwell, had her great idea, upon which she consulted the Soho-born Inspector McCarthy.

She had been, she informed him, a saving woman whose personal wants were few. To her had come the idea of redecorating the pin-table blot upon the Sohoan landscape and opening it as a café for the respectable tradesmen of the neighbourhood, where cooking of the best, and wines of a sound quality, would be procurable at a price to suit the pockets of her neighbours.

McCarthy hailed the idea with enthusiasm; interviewed the landlord upon the signora's behalf and knocked the rent down by nearly fifty per cent, after expatiating at some length to that gentleman upon what a splendid thing it would be for him to realize that he owned at least *one* piece of property which the police would unhesitatingly class as eminently respectable. So very different to the rest of his possessions in the quarter, which authority relegated to a totally different class, and which might quite easily become the object of unheralded police investigation at any moment.

The inspector's argument worked like a charm. In less than one month from that conversation all traces of the disreputable pin-table dive had disappeared and the *Café Milano* (Lucia Spadoglia, Ltd.) opened its hospitable doors.

But there was one fly in the signora's ointment, though the knowledgeable inspector had foreseen it: the erstwhile patrons of the pin-tables saw in the signora's enterprise a magnificent opportunity for free, and unlimited meals. Here was an establishment which to them was as manna from Heaven! Only a woman in charge; not even a doorman to be dealt with—though he would promptly have been given the "broken glass" treatment had he shown any sign of obstreperousness.

Upon the opening night the "boys" were there in full strength and soon were well under way. The respectable patrons present to honour the occasion looked askance; some stole quietly away before the trouble started. The signora, as became a woman of courage and enterprise, faced it all without the move of a muscle.

Then suddenly arrived a supper party of sixteen, headed by Patron Number One, Detective-Inspector McCarthy. His guests were composed entirely of units of the *personnel* of New Scotland Yard and a hard, splendidly-conditioned lot they looked. The fall of a pin would have sounded like a thud in the silence which reigned as the inspector and his party took their seats at two tables reserved for them nearby the cash desk at which the signora presided.

The gang being at that time under the leadership of the well-known and rightly-feared Mo Eberstein, the inspector invited that gentleman into an adjacent room for a few words. What exactly transpired has never to this day been made public by either party, but the appearance of the gang-boss suggested that he had not seen eye to eye with the inspector. Both his were bunged tight and rapidly assuming all the colours of the spectrum as McCarthy guided him to the door; the rest of his not really pleasant features were quite unrecognizable.

Before midnight the word had fairly swept through Soho that any member of the gangs who so much as looked cock-eyed at the exterior of the *Café Milano*, let alone the inside, could prepare for personal trouble from Detective-Inspector

McCarthy, and in large and ever-increasing doses. It was plenty: from that night the enterprise of the signora had never looked back.

For some twenty minutes now the inspector had been waiting the coming of the person with whom he had a supper appointment, and had spent that interval studying the patrons, regular and casual. Of the former there were fewer than usual, since, nowadays, Soho does not live over its places of business to the same extent as of yore, and the tendency of the black-out was to send suburban dwellers home at the earliest possible moment.

Nor was the casual trade improved by the necessary gloom; to get through Soho streets from either Oxford Street or Shaftesbury Avenue to the well-advertised *Café Milano*, which was situated about midway between them, was a job, these nights, to make even the stoutest heart flinch.

There were, as in most places of the kind, a fair sprinkling of those refugees, mostly Austrians, drinking that coffee topped by a good inch of whipped cream so dear to the Viennese, two or three tables of Italian business men drinking flasked Chianti with their modest meal and, he could hear, discussing with profound relief the neutrality of the Italian government in the war.

There were also a few groups of sad-looking Germans, people he knew personally to be of long residence in this country, and for the greater part naturalized, and whose sympathy with the aims and ideology of Nazi Germany were absolutely *nil*.

And then his eyes fell upon one man seated at a single table alone, before him a liqueur which, by the look of his table, was the finishing touch to one of the signora's most excellent suppers.

In appearance he was a rather singular mixture of colouring; olive-skinned rather than swarthy, with raven-black almost varnished-looking hair and exceptionally white teeth which he showed perpetually in a rather supercilious smile. Not that any of these physiological points were in any way uncommon in Soho. As far as they went McCarthy could have found a hundred similar in a five minutes' walk. Nothing to hold the eye about them. But the eyes of the man were a totally different thing. They were, without exception, the very lightest shade of blue that the inspector ever remembered to have seen; they were an almost ice-blue, and from the angle at which he watched them they seemed to carry a greenish tinge.

As the man sat, apparently staring at the wall and lost in thought, they seemed to have no expression whatever. They struck him as being of a fixed rigidity—just as are the eyes of a snake who stares through glass with unblinking fixity at an interested visitor to the snake-house at the Zoo. So utterly expressionless did they appear to be, that for a moment McCarthy could almost fancy that the man was blind.

He was well dressed, exceptionally so in comparison with the company present, but to one who prided himself upon his knowledge of matters sartorial, his clothes were obviously not of English cut. There was about them that indefinable, but very definite difference which exists between the art of the best English tailors and their Continental brethren of the same status.

"Now I wonder who th' divil you are," McCarthy apostrophized the perfectly still figure. "You're not Soho, or even temporarily resident here. I'll stake my life on that."

The theory that those queer, staring, and utterly expressionless eyes were sightless was exploded when their owner, snapping suddenly out of the deep reverie in which he had been sunk, beckoned to him one of the two little waitresses who were recent additions to the signora's *ménage*. From her he took his bill, paid it with what, from the flush of pleasure which came into the girl's face, must have been a handsome tip. He stood up and then took an overcoat which hung upon the wall near his table, down from its peg.

He was a tall man, six feet in his stockinged feet McCarthy would have put him down as, and had to stoop considerably before the little waitress could get the coat across the broad shoulders. A fine figure of a man, McCarthy granted instantly; clean limbed and as alert as they come, or he was no judge—for all those strange, unmoving eyes.

That he was gently-bred was proved by the bow he gave the girl as he took his hat from her, and also the military bend of his body he gave to the signora as he moved towards the door. There was something in the very leisureliness of his walk, as he moved along the carpeted passages between the tables, which was almost insolent; as if inwardly he was smiling contemptuously at the simple place in which he found himself, and the equally simple people who patronized it. Just for one moment he paused at the door—to take from his overcoat pocket a small torch which he switched on.

As his hand moved towards the handle, the door suddenly opened to admit the person for whom Inspector McCarthy had been waiting—Assistant Commissioner of Police (C) Sir William Haynes. The man with the strange eyes politely dropped back a step until Sir William had entered, then passed out into the inky night.

Chapter II

Detective-Inspector McCarthy
Discourses of Things and People

"Exactly twenty-two minutes," the inspector greeted accusingly.

"Eh!" Sir William exclaimed, as he divested himself of his overcoat and hat and handed them over to the second of the small waitresses. "Twenty-two minutes late, I suppose you mean. My dear Mac, you're lucky that it's not forty. With all due respect to the A.R.P. people, the black-out is the very devil."

The signora came forward from her cash desk to give proper greetings to her second star patron.

"I hope I haven't messed everything up, Signora," he apologized, "but getting from—from our place of business on the Embankment to here has been an almost impossible job."

"Ever't'ing weel be-a just ready, Signori," the signora informed them with her gracious smile. "These-a days I always allowa time for-a da black-out. People, they notta can com' just-a to time."

"By gad, and that's a fact," the A.C. exclaimed. "Bally lucky to get here at all if they're in our job. Ready, when you are, Signora—more than ready."

"I've been that for the last twenty minutes," the inspector mentioned, more to the ceiling than any particular person present. "A divil of a lot of sympathy I get for it. It's always the way. 'Tis the poor that..."

The Assistant Commissioner smiled.

"...that helps the poor, or perhaps it's that 'bears the brunt of the burden' this time. One or other of them."

"Both," McCarthy returned equably. "Did y' notice that chap who went out as you came in, Bill?"

Haynes nodded. "Couldn't very well help it. Queer-looking bird, rather. Strange eyes—for a moment I thought he was blind. Who is he? One of your Soho clients?"

McCarthy shook his head negatively.

"To the best of my belief I've never set eyes on him in my life before. But he's certainly a bit out of the ordinary rut—to look at, anyhow. I just wondered if you'd run across him before. The West End is full of some queer people, these days."

Sir William sighed. "You're telling *me*, as the Americans say," he said feelingly. "I've just been having two solid hours with one of them in my room. A little gent brought in by the S.B. men for questioning."

"One of the merry little spy lads?" McCarthy asked interestedly.

"Yes; and one of the old hands at that. You've never heard such a convincing rigmarole as he'd got all cut and dried and polished up, ready for English consumption. According to him he was an Austrian Social Democrat and had escaped out of a concentration camp to this country, and what he hadn't been through in the way of physical torture was nobody's business. The only thing against that tale was that, beyond a few old scars, he hadn't a mark on his face, but before we knew where we were he had peeled off his shirt and shown us his back. There were plenty of marks there to bear out his statement, but, unfortunately for him, you didn't need to be a doctor to know that they were of a good many years' standing. Anyhow, I let him go on and go on."

"Gave him enough rope to hang himself?" McCarthy suggested.

"We didn't need that," Haynes said. "My memory, plus our excellent *dossier* system, was all we needed. He was about as much Austrian as I am. As it happened, my memory was better than his, for I remembered running the rule over him very definitely in the Great War. He was a much younger man then, of course, and a Belgian refugee from Antwerp in those days. His tale didn't save him then, and let him down again this time. He's at Cannon Street station at the present moment, on his way to an internment camp." He chuckled at some memory which had evidently amused him.

"What's the joke?" McCarthy asked.

"You should have heard him give us his own private Hymn of Hate when he realized that it was no good and that he was booked." Sir William laughed. "Man, if everything he promised us comes true there won't be any England left in a fortnight. We're going to be bombed right clean off the map, every man-jack of us, and black-outs and A.R.P. and anti-aircraft defences won't save us. The U-boats are going to put our Navy, as well as our Mercantile Marine craft, down on the bed of the sea inside six weeks—except such cargoes as they'll take into the German ports, of course. Our civil population are going to be taken *en masse* as slaves to Poland, to re-build that devastated country under the lash, and…and the Lord knows what else. It was as good as circus while it lasted."

"'Tis you that get all the fun while I'm prowling the streets with me little torch," McCarthy observed. "All the same, Bill, there are plenty of these gentry, and their *femina*—don't forget the ladies—who aren't all hot air, though they've plenty of hate about them, who can do a devil of a lot of mischief if ever they're given the chance."

"Not a doubt of that," Haynes agreed seriously. "And the worst of it is, Mac, that the most dangerous of them are of a totally different class and well equipped for their job in every way. They're not snooping round, all ears to hear what they can in cafés, or bars frequented by men of the Services. They're people who are mixing with the higher-ups, the folks who do get odd bits of information out of Whitehall and the Civil Services, generally. The people that you daren't lay a hand on without some bigwig rushing around declaring that it's a scandal, not to say a crime, that such excellent people should have an eye kept on them, not to mention be questioned."

"Now that's the beauty of my particular 'clients' in Soho," McCarthy said with a smile of satisfaction. "If you've the belief that any of them are taking base gold in payment for that sort of work, ye can lug them out and put the fear of God into them without anyone rushing round to the Houses of Parliament, or anywhere else, to put in a good word for them. Which, as half my particular lot would sell their own mothers for a bob, is perhaps just as well."

As he spoke the door opened and one unmistakable product of Soho entered.

He was a tall, slim, but powerfully built young man, in years anything from six and twenty to thirty, with the dark olive skin, heavily lashed black eyes, and raven-hued, sleek hair which pronounced him instantly to be Soho-Italian—in all probability London-born of Italian parents. His clothes were of the best, though about them, generally, there was a certain raffishness of cut, helped by the black felt hat he wore pulled down over his eyes in a manner that suggested certain mask-like uses when occasion demanded.

There was an expression of predatoriness not to be missed in the black eyes which switched instantly to the inspector, and a tightness about the mouth which seemed to say that its owner, despite his sleek appearance, was a person it was not wise to run foul of. A large and extremely glittering diamond ornamented one finger of his right hand, whilst a similar stone radiated its sparkling light from his tie-pin. Taken all in all the newcomer might have been accepted as typical of the present-day West End gangster, the greater part of whose daylight activities were relegated to the racecourses and kindred pursuits, while his nights were given up to still more unholy activities in and around the cafés and dance-halls of Soho.

With one quick lift of his eye-lids, McCarthy took him in, then went on with the very excellent supper the signora had provided.

But, strangely enough, this colourful young man, although his first glance had been towards the table not so long since vacated by the man with the ice-blue eyes, stopped and markedly divested himself of his hat and over-coat, which he carefully hung up upon the hat-stand which stood but a foot or so from Inspector McCarthy's elbow. As he did so, a tiny ball of paper, so small that it might have been a cigarette paper rolled up, dropped from his hand to the inspector's table where it lay within an inch of that officer's plate. Without as much as a glance in its direction, the young man moved across to the table he had first marked with his eyes; by the time he had reached it, the tiny ball of paper had disappeared.

"Who is the tough-looking laddie?" the Assistant Commissioner asked in an undertone.

"A certain 'client,'" McCarthy answered in the same way. "Not so tough as he looks, Bill, if it really comes to it—unless of course he has his gang with him, and then he's definitely bad meat. But, like most of them, on his own as harmless as a chicken. A nasty bit of work," the inspector went on, "in fact, what you might call a messy job altogether. I don't like using such people, and do so as little as I can help it, but there are times when it is absolutely necessary for a man in our game to get what the little birds are whispering in places not so easy to get into. Though there aren't many that I don't breeze into like a brother in full benefit."

"I see," Haynes said. "He's one of those 'little birds' you often quote as whispering things to you. Who is he?"

"His name is Mascagni—Floriello Mascagni," McCarthy informed him.

"That name is familiar to me somewhere," Haynes said frowningly.

"If ye're under any impression that he is any connection of *the* Mascagni—Pietro I think the name is, but I wouldn't swear to it—get it out of your mind at once. He's not; far from it. I'm referring, of course, to the one who gave us *Madame Butterfly*, and other beautiful operas. There's nothing of the butterfly about Flo. Mascagni. Divil a bit. In his own way he's about as dirty a tyke as you'd come across in a day's walk, but there are occasions when he is useful to me, and this is one of them."

"Dangerous game for him, isn't it?" Haynes questioned.

"Not the healthiest in the world, I'll admit," McCarthy answered placidly. "But if a man is a born crook and double-crosser he's going to sell valuable information to someone, sooner or later, and it might just as well be me as anyone else. But one of these days, Bill, they'll tumble to him and someone will wipe a *chiv* across his throat as sure as we're sitting here. Well, at the worst, it'll get rid of a damn pest, and at the best, it'll save the country the expense of trying and hanging him. Which suits me admirably."

"It's a strange thing, Mac, that crime and particularly crimes of violence have dropped to practically nothing since war. Just a few hoodlums rough-housing about in the black-out, but nothing serious. In this infernal gloom you'd have thought that they'd have been at it with a vengeance, particularly at this end of the town."

McCarthy's eyes twinkled. "Most of the younger ones are busy conferring as to the best way to get together and kill the Sergeant Major," he observed whimsically. "The rest of them are thinking up their spiel for the tribunals, when they appear as Conscientious Objectors to violence of any sort or kind. It's a queer world, Bill, and there's some damn funny folk live in it."

"And this particular part of it has its fair share of them."

"As one of the denizens of this particular quarter, being born in it and reared in its gutters, I take exception to that remark," the inspector said with a grin. "It's no worse, and no better, than any other part of London where you've got a mixed population. There are as many entirely respectable people living in Soho as there are in Streatham—though I'm bound to admit," he emended, "that they don't take life as seriously there as they do here. And if they're a bit too inclined to say it with a knife, instead of music, or flowers, you mustn't forget that's hereditary, and a strongly-embedded racial characteristic. They can't be altogether blamed for that. Anyhow," he concluded dryly, "it keeps the police division operating this district well up on their toes, and that's something. Just a minute until I read my mail."

With a dexterous flip of his fingers which showed how used he was to receiving communications of this kind, and without even glancing at it as he did it, McCarthy opened the tiny slip of paper which had been dropped upon the table by Mascagni. When opened he cast one glance at it, to read, and memorize, a certain name and address. After which he tore the scrap of paper into such tiny fragments that not even the most diligent could ever have put them together again.

"Yes," he observed almost sadly to his friend, "it will be the *chiv* for our twisty little friend Floriello one of these days. Nothing in the world more certain than that!"

The inspector stood up, and seemingly, fiddled about in his overcoat pocket from which he eventually withdrew his cigarette case. When again he seated himself there, a couple of treasury notes found their way, as though by sleight of hand, into the overcoat pocket of Mr. Floriello Mascagni.

It was very nearly midnight when Sir William Haynes and McCarthy made their way out into the black night again; the latter whistled for a cab, but in vain.

"You won't get one about here, sir, I'm afraid," a constable who turned up upon the scene informed him. "It takes them all they know to pick up fares in the main thoroughfares."

"Then there's nothing for it but to grope my way to Bloomsbury," the Assistant Commissioner said, with a wry smile which no one could see.

"That's the worst of coming out suppering with you, Mac, it's the getting home afterwards, these nights."

"The Lord be thanked I'm different," McCarthy said virtuously. "I don't put on dog and live in a mansion in a Bloomsbury square. I live near my food and my 'clients.' If the worst comes to the worst I can always get home to my bed on my hands and knees.

"And talking about bed," he observed, "when I get into mine to-night I'm not going to get out of it again for any-body. The spies can go on spying and the murderers can go on murdering, but upon this night Patrick Aloysius

McCarthy is going to get his fair share of shut-eye, if he never has it again."

"Is that to be taken as meaning that you'll refuse duty if you're called out?" Sir William said with a laugh.

"Consider it refused in advance. Good night—and don't lose yourself between here and Bedford Square. The Yard would never get over the loss."

Chapter III

The Scream in the Black-Out

Opinions in that particular portion of Soho in which the crime was committed differed as to the exact quality of the terrible scream that rang out at five minutes past one, precisely. Police Constable C. 1285, working a Soho beat, part of which forced him to inch himself through the gloom from Oxford Street the length of Dean Street to Shaftesbury Avenue, was positive that it came from the throat of a woman; anyhow, it stopped him dead. For a scream in the early hours of the morning in Soho, even from a female throat, to stop dead in his tracks a hard-boiled constable who had worked in that cosmopolitan quarter for years, had to be something entirely out of the ordinary, as, indeed, this one was!

He was passing the short entry into Soho Square at the time, and the sound came from the left of him; that is to say from the direction of the square itself. Male or female, it undoubtedly came from the throat of a person in mortal terror and, to judge by the curious gurgling note upon which it finished, the sound had been stopped by someone other than the screamer.

On the other hand, Detective Inspector McCarthy, but an hour or so after leaving Sir William Haynes, and at that moment in the act of switching out his light before stepping into bed, was very positive that the scream came from the throat of a man. Not a matter, it might be thought, of any great moment, but should that scream which penetrated the Cimmerian blackness herald a case of murder, as it certainly sounded to do, it could be of considerable consequence.

The inspector promptly flung up the window of his bedroom which fronted on to Dean Street, and peered out in the direction from which the sound had seemed to him to come. For all he could see he might just as well have switched out his light and peered under the bed.

Pulling an overcoat over his night attire and slipping an automatic pistol hurriedly into its pocket, he groped his way downstairs and was out in that thoroughfare in his slippered feet almost before the echoes of that ghastly sound had died away. To him, also, the direction from which the cry came seemed to be Soho Square, towards which he groped at such speed as he could make, thumbing back the safety-catch of his automatic as he went. The thing he had forgotten to bring was the one most necessary of all—his torch.

The windows of flats and other lodgings situated above the shops of Dean Street were being flung up rapidly, and heads of people not usually disturbed by such sounds were being thrust out of them. Not that they could see anything, any more than anyone could see them, but it is to be supposed that they got a certain amount of satisfaction from their futile effort to penetrate the impenetrable. Which served to show still more the terrible quality of that cry when, even in a neighbourhood where midnight screams were no strange sound, this one was unhesitatingly set down as an accompaniment, prelude would perhaps be the better word, to murder.

Just how many times in his career McCarthy had boasted that he could traverse Soho at any hour of the day or night blindfolded, or in the thickest fog, was borne in weightily upon him at this moment. Fog was one thing, and bad enough in the congested streets of Soho to rattle anyone. But this never-to-be-sufficiently-damned black-out business was the absolute frozen limit! For the safety of the populace it was necessary, he supposed, and therefore had to be endured, but how the divil any man was supposed to get quickly upon the track of crime committed in it was something more than he was prepared to answer.

His first crash was into a light standard which received the shock without murmur; his second was into someone who gave indignant tongue in a manner to which the word "murmur" could certainly not be applied.

By the feel of the obstacle it was the front of an extremely stout Italian lady who cursed him fluently in what McCarthy instantly recognized as the Neapolitan idiom of his dead mother. It was interlarded with many calls upon the *Madonna mia*, and many other of the better known saints of her native land. Uttering in the same tongue the soft, appeasing words which, we are told, turneth away wrath, and in which the lady recognized instantly the voice of the Detective Inspector McCarthy that staggered officer reassured her. She apologized handsomely and sent the inspector upon his way with the cheering personal opinion that the lads of either the *Mafia or Camorrista* were at it again!

At the corner leading into the square itself, McCarthy also bumped into C. 1285 who, all things considered, was also showing a fair turn of speed. He recognized the voice of the inspector instantly—aided possibly by the quality of some of the adjectives he was using.

"Where?" McCarthy snapped, when he, in turn, recognized the voice of the bumped.

"It seemed to me to come from the square, sir. By heaven, it was an awful scream!"

Into the square and round it the pair crawled, to find the windows of such places of residence as are still left there well up, and presumably filled with a wondering and shuddering audience. For the rest of it, the square might have been a large expanse of black velvet, for anything that could be seen in it.

At that moment there occurred one of those happenings which the inspector was wont to refer to as "the Luck of the McCarthys." For all that, at the moment and in the circumstances, it might have seemed to him a manifestation of a beneficent Providence, to other persons concerned, such as the owner of the premises, the A.R.P. authorities and the fire brigades, it probably took on a totally different aspect. These things all depend upon the point of view.

At any rate, and without the slightest warning, a sheet of flame burst suddenly from the roof of one of the few old tenement houses left standing in the vicinity of the square, though rather back from it. It later transpired that some attic dweller, aroused from slumber by that ghastly scream, had darted out of bed in a more or less bemused state and knocked over a paraffin lamp which, despite superhuman struggle, promptly had the place in flames. Although the efforts of the firemen managed to prevent it spreading to other nearby buildings, the one in question was eventually gutted, and in the process lit the square and those who rushed into it almost with the searching light of day. It amazed the inspector to find how many hundreds of people had managed to find their way into it, and as for the audience at the surrounding upper windows, their name was legion.

By this time the pounding of heavy feet along the pavements and the constant shrilling of police whistles told both McCarthy and C. 1285 that further official assistance was upon the way. In the next few moments their force was augmented by a panting sergeant accompanied by two uniformed men; another minute saw that number enlarged by a still further force of both uniformed and plain-clothed men. McCarthy promptly took charge.

"Beat the square, every inch of it," he ordered. "And lose no time about it. In a minute or two we'll have the brigades here and what in the way of clues they don't trample out of sight for ever, they'll hose to blazes! Grab any person that looks in the least suspicious and hold them for interrogation."

But although his orders were carried out with extraordinary alacrity and such thoroughness that scarcely a pin dropped upon the pavement would have been missed, and, additionally, was got through before the first of the fire engines roared their way into the square, not one sign of anything appertaining to murder in any shape or form had there been found.

"Well, this beats Bannagher, and he beat the divil!" McCarthy muttered to himself. "We'll try the entrance to the square," he said to the sergeant. "It was from there that cry came, I'm more than positive."

"I'd have thought so myself," that grizzled officer returned perplexedly. "Though, mind you, Inspector, I was at the Oxford Street corner of Soho Street when I heard it. But that's where I'd have said it came from."

In the lurid light of the now fast-rising flames, they searched every doorway on their left hand, but it was not until they came to the deeply-recessed entrance of the last of the historic residences left of a time when Soho Square was as fashionable a place of residence as Berkeley Square is to-day, that they came across unmistakable signs of what they sought.

Two old and well-worn stone steps led up to a magnif-icently-carved and pillared doorway, above which was an ornate fanlight, carved in the centre with the date 1702. The lintels and the pillars supporting the porch were painted in a deep green, but the door itself was spotless white—except where both lintel and lower panels were liberally bedaubed with blood, some of which still slowly trickled down the smoothness of the heavily enamelled woodwork! In the light of the fire it looked like black ink, but not to the experienced eyes which gave it their keen survey.

The two worn wells in the centre of the old stone steps were literally little pools of blood which had splashed as far as the ornamental fencing, fronting stone steps which again led down to a basement. Turning the sergeant's torch down there, McCarthy let out a gasp, and before anyone realized what he was at had darted down the steps to pick up gingerly a long three-edged stiletto, the blade of which was thick with blood!

That the weapon was of foreign origin he was positive. Near it, and caught in a piece of wire-netting which had been suspended above part of the basement for some purpose, was a tiny square of linen, surrounded by deep, but very fine, lace; a woman's handkerchief. It, too, was heavily spotted with blood. But of the victim of what was obviously a ghastly and blood-thirsty crime there was no sign whatever!

Chapter IV

McCarthy Follows a "Hunch"

By the time the inspector had made these gruesome discoveries, a veritable avalanche of people, drawn as much by the fire as the thrilling, fast-spreading rumour of murder, or more likely the wholly-entertaining combination of both, had descended upon the square from every angle. Despite the efforts of the uniformed men, now strongly reinforced, they had hard work to keep the morbidly curious from off the heels of even McCarthy, himself. That officer beckoned the sergeant to him.

"Don't let 'em be too busy at that, Sergeant," he said quietly. "It's as likely as not that the one responsible for this may be among that lot. It wouldn't be the first time that the person who's done a job of this sort has mingled with the crowd to watch events. Just keep them out of my pocket and that'll do. I'm keeping my eyes wide open."

But with all the evidences of a ghastly death which were there plainly to be seen, one thing fogged McCarthy completely. Here upon the step and actual door of this old residence, now, by the way, cut up into sets of offices, used for the greater part by legal men and business agents for foreign importers, was every trace of a terrible crime. But there those traces stopped dead; upon the pavement itself there was not as much as a drop of blood.

"It almost looks, sir," the sergeant whispered, "as though whoever committed the murder had opened the door and dragged the body inside."

"Ye won't mind my mentioning the fact that we're only *pre-supposing* a killing, Sergeant," McCarthy pointed out. "To have a *bona fide* murder you must have a corpse, the body must be produced at any subsequent festivities, and up to now there's no sign of one."

"There's all the signs I'd want," the sergeant said flatly. "Not to mention that scream."

"And how do you know," McCarthy said, "that some foul brute in a lust of cruelty hasn't cut a dog's throat to account for all this blood, then thrust it in a bag and carted it off?"

"A dog doesn't scream like a tortured soul for one thing, nor does it use expensive-looking lace handkerchiefs like the one you found on that wire," the sergeant argued stubbornly.

McCarthy nodded. "True; true. Such evidence as is before us suggests a woman in the case. So, you think, does that scream. I'm not so sure of that. But I'm still pointing out to you that until we find a body we're pre-supposing a murder. Though, mind you, again I'll admit freely that such evidence as we have is all in favour of the idea."

The sergeant gave a quick glance at him. Although he had known Detective Inspector McCarthy practically ever since he had left the uniformed force for the Yard, he had never come in contact with him on a case. Rumour said that the inspector, albeit as clever as paint and a man who was bound for the top of the tree fast, was not only as mad as a hatter, but an inveterate joker under any circumstances. With the incontestable evidence of murder plainly in front of his eyes, not to mention that scream still ringing in his ears, the sergeant found himself wondering whether that uncrushable sense of humour he had heard of was at work again, with himself for the goat.

But what little of the inspector's face he could see showed no signs of anything but frowning perplexity; certainly there was nothing of humour lightening it at that particular moment.

"And," Inspector McCarthy went on thoughtfully, "we're also taking it for granted that the killer was a man, principally because in this delightful part of the world when there's any murdering done it's generally men who do it and women usually the objects of their attention. And, once more, the evidence of that handkerchief is entirely in favour of that deduction. Yet it may be leading us entirely astray."

"How could it do that, Inspector?" the sergeant questioned. "There is the handkerchief and the dagger…"

"Stiletto," McCarthy corrected. "Not a weapon to be commonly found in Soho. Knives in plenty, as I've no doubt you and the rest of the lads of the C. Division know as well as I do. I don't doubt that you've had to intervene in a fair number of knife fights in your time."

"Plenty," the sergeant answered promptly. "And an ugly job it is too, when their blood is up and they mean business."

McCarthy nodded his agreement; he had had his fair share of that most ungentle pastime as well.

"But," he continued, "I doubt very much if you saw a weapon of the type I found here in any of their hands, Sergeant?"

"No, I can't say that I have. It looks a fancy sort of thing to me."

"That's just it," the inspector said. "A stiletto of that type, small, three-edged and pointed, is invariably the kind of weapon that the ladies hug to their bosoms. Which is all right as long as they don't drive it into someone else—which they're just as likely to do as not, if worked up sufficiently over an affair of the heart gone wrong, rabid jealousy or some soul-searing business of that kind. It's the kind of weapon they can keep handily tucked in their bodices, blouses or whatever they call 'em. I've even known them appear with startling suddenness out of their garters before to-day."

"I never thought of that," the sergeant said, somewhat lamely. "Come to think of it, it *is* more a woman's weapon than a man's."

"And then," McCarthy pursued, "we have Exhibit B—the handkerchief. Why should it not be just as much the property of the murderer as the murdered? The odds are fifty-fifty with a slight shade in favour of its belonging to the murderer—murderess in that case, of course."

"Damned if I can see that," the sergeant grunted. The inspector's deductions were getting a bit too involved for him.

"Simply because ninety-nine times out of a hundred, murder committed by a woman is a *crime passionel*, and while she is on the job everything else has gone from her mind. She's far more likely to leave damnable evidence of her guilt behind her than any man is. No matter what may be at the bottom of his killing, he's thinking of himself first, last, and all of the time; it's generally by some well-thought-out bloomer that he's convicted. However, I'm not being didactic about it, I'm simply pointing out to you that until we find the corpse it's an even chance either way."

The sergeant made no response, but the thought passed through his mind that there was not much of this "mad as a hatter" stuff noticeable about the inspector when he was expounding a deduction.

Borrowing the sergeant's torch again, he turned it upon the handle of the door.

"You'll notice, Sergeant, that there's not as much as a mark on the handle of this door to suggest that anyone concerned in this sticky business opened it?"

"Been wiped perhaps," the sergeant suggested.

McCarthy shook his head. "If it had had as much as a drop of blood on it and been wiped, it would show a smear; as it is, it's perfectly clean; only dulled a bit in the course of the day's usage. However, we won't take chances, there may be 'dabs' on it when it's gone over properly."

Taking out his handkerchief, he wrapped it around the handle and tried the door. It was locked.

"I think I'm right when I say that there's no caretaker to this particular lot of offices?"

"None," the sergeant said. "There are a couple of old women who come in about six o'clock in the evening and clean up the place. They shut the door after them. There's a bit of a lad who gets here about eight o'clock in the morning, opens up, and puts the post in its proper receptacles before the others arrive. As far as I know, that's all the staff there is here."

McCarthy applied the torch to the keyhole and studied it intently.

"Without being positive I'm fairly certain this has never been touched recently," he said. "Though how the person, or whatever was killed, was got off the ground in the space of time that it *must* have been, has got me licked. There's only one way that I can think of at the moment, and that's a car."

The sergeant shook his head.

"I doubt they had a chance to have got anyone from this step into a car and run out of the square between the time that scream was heard and we got to it. Not in the black-out and without being heard. And don't forget," he added, "that the men on beat in this particular part of Oxford Street, and also the Charing Cross Road, heard the scream, and they would have been on the look-out for anything that came out of the square. With a sound like that in their ears they'd have taken a chance and pulled up anything on wheels."

As the inspector listened his eyes were wandering with apparent casualness over the fire-lit crowd which had gathered. Most of them were Sohoans, and for the greater part of foreign extraction, but there were also a few late birds who had hurried in from the main thoroughfares to satisfy their curiosity.

Most of them were well-known to McCarthy, many of them honest, hard-working people, for the greater part employees of the restaurants and hotels of the West End. But there were also others whose hard and furtive eyes told of very different ways of earning a living; men known to him as gangsters and depredators of the most vicious type. And as they caught his eyes upon them, their glances shifted quickly and they unostentatiously dropped out of view.

But, somehow, he had the feeling that they had no hand in this business. This murder, if murder it proved to be, was too cunningly conceived for any of them. The whole business was too unusual, had been too cleverly worked for him to have any suspicion of them being concerned in it. Their methods were wicked enough in all conscience, but never by any stretch of imagination brainy. And, besides, that stiletto had not been a thing to be picked up for a few shillings, or a few pounds for the matter of that; he would not be at all surprised to find that it was an antique weapon of very considerable value, while if some expert in such matters did not inform him that the lace handkerchief was an extremely pricey article, far beyond the means of the average lady of Soho, he would be a much mistaken man.

Others there were, too, who had drifted into the square for no other reason than the fire and the whisper which had shot around. They were certainly not of Soho or, for the matter of that, of either of the preceding classes. Men in evening dress covered by overcoats, in some cases accompanied by women; late scholars from some private bottle parties or, still more likely, from some of the "underground" night clubs which still flourished, despite either the black-out, or the earnest efforts of the authorities.

He was about to turn back to the door again when his eyes fell upon one person standing at the corner of the actual square itself; a person whose presence there gave him quite a shock, though why it should have done so was more than he could have explained to himself or anyone else. It was the man with the ice-blue eyes who had left the *Café Milano* at the very moment of Bill Haynes' entrance. Singularly enough those queerly-compelling eyes of his seemed, in the lurid glow cast by the fire, to be lighter than ever—they stood out from the man's immobile face almost like those of a cat in the dark.

And, moreover—that it might have been pure imagination upon his part he conceded freely—the man's mouth, albeit the rest of his face seemed to express nothing at all, appeared to be twisted into a supercilious smile. It was almost as though he might be saying to himself, as he watched the efforts of McCarthy and the sergeant: "Look at those two benighted idiots; what do they think they are going to accomplish between them?"

Out of the corner of his eye he saw the man approach the constable engaged in keeping the crowd back at the corner of the square and put what was evidently a question to him. The constable, McCarthy could see, answered it civilly, and with a curt nod of acknowledgment the questioner turned and moved slowly, and with that almost insolent gait of his, in the direction of Charing Cross Road. Which was the last McCarthy saw of him, for at that moment a squad-car swung into the square from the same direction and pulled up within a few feet of him, cutting the man out of his vision. From it there alighted McCarthy's own superintendent, accompanied by his chief-inspector, and as murder in the Division was up to the former, McCarthy was ready for his superior to take over, there and then.

Giving that overworked official a short but detailed account of what had taken place, he concluded his report by saying that as the superintendent would doubtless wish to take hold of the case he, personally, would be off back to his bed and endeavour to make up such of the time he had lost.

But Superintendent Burman shook his head. "I don't think so, Mac," he said. "Since you've been in this right from the beginning, you may as well see it through. In any case I'm going away for a conference to-morrow, and I'm not letting this or anything else break into it. So you can go ahead with a satisfied mind that you'll get no interference from me."

Which was, in Inspector McCarthy's opinion, a good hearing; very definitely so. The "Sooper" was a good sort, but a man of old-fashioned methods and hide-bound with Red-tape and Regulations. If McCarthy was any judge of a case from its first leads, this was going to be one which called for something very different to the routine stuff Superintendent Burman would not only have applied to it himself, but would, if advising, have seen that the officer in charge did as well.

"I tackle this on my own lines, sir?" he asked quickly.

The superintendent eyed him askance for a moment. "Within reasonable bounds, McCarthy, yes, of course. But," he added, sternly, "I hope you'll employ none of those lone-handed methods of yours that, nine times out of ten, are as illegal as anything the criminals you're chasing have done."

"I wouldn't dream of anything of the kind, sir," the inspector answered mildly.

"Well, is there anything we can do?" the "Sooper" asked, agreeably surprised by this emollient answer.

"Yes!" McCarthy snapped, a very different note in his voice. "Have this square cleared and lend me your car for a few minutes."

Before there could be any possible refusal of the latter request, he was inside the vehicle, shouted an order at its driver, and it was poking its nose through the crowd on its way towards Charing Cross Road.

"Take it calm and quiet," he said to the squad-car driver. "There's a certain party just left the square that I want to pick up without letting him have the faintest suspicion that he's being followed, if you get the idea?"

"A suspect in this case, Inspector?" the chauffeur asked eagerly. Although his principal business was shooting that car along at any pace, legal or otherwise, that whoever it was in it might request, he was as much up on his toes when there was a good murder about as the next man wearing uniform.

But, although usually the soul of affability to all and sundry, and particularly those beneath him in official status, the inspector did not answer the query—as a matter of fact he was quite pertinently asking himself another.

"Now what the divil am I following this fellow up for?" he questioned himself acutely. "Beyond that I saw him once before to-night and his appearance interested me, I know nothing whatever about him. At the very moment that my duty demands that I ought to be poking my nose into that area and trying to read something useful into the stiletto and handkerchief I've got in my pocket, here I go leaving the ground and off on this wild-goose chase. There's no sense in it; it's just one of those damned senseless 'hunches' of mine which may lead anywhere—and most likely nowhere. The very thing I've just been cautioned by my superior officer against doing, and here I am at it almost before he's got the words out of his mouth! These infernal 'hunches' of mine will be my downfall."

Chapter V

In Which the Tragedy Deepens

Notwithstanding this gloomy prognostication, the inspector settled himself down in the vehicle and kept a sharp eye upon both sides of Charing Cross Road. His eyes getting used to the gloom, he suddenly caught sight of his man heading in a westerly direction along Oxford Street. But McCarthy noted that although he was moving along at that usual leisurely pace of his at the moment, he must have travelled at a good speed to have got where he was in the time that he had.

Once—it was just after he had passed Berners Street—his quarry stopped dead and swung round sharply, peering into the road. There was nothing to be seen but the dimmed light of a belated taxi and the squad-car which, on McCarthy's instructions, kept well to the centre of the road. At the latter he looked intently for a moment.

"Now, I wonder if those queer eyes of yours saw this wagon come into the square?" McCarthy apostrophized the figure. "They look the sort that don't miss much, for all they've as much life in them as those of a corpse. If they did, it's not much good my wasting time following you up in it, and, moreover, it's going to arouse suspicion in you, which is the last thing I want."

On went the man again, leaving McCarthy in a quandary. He would have followed the job up on foot but for the fact that, clad as he was in a somewhat startling dressing-gown and slippers, he certainly was not going to get very far without the man realizing who was following him. And all the time the profound and disturbing feeling was growing upon him that no line of argument he could put forward could justify him in any way for wasting further time upon this utterly unknown man.

But McCarthy was nothing if not stubborn, and having started out to follow a hunch he was loath indeed to alter his plan. However, in the circumstances, he saw nothing else for it and he was about to tell his driver to turn and make back for Soho Square and routine when his eye caught sight of a shadowy figure skulking out of Oxford Street into an alley which led behind a certain row of shop premises. In an instant McCarthy's eagle eye had penetrated the gloom sufficiently to identify the amorphous shape. Even under these difficult circumstances he could not be mistaken in him as one of his regular "clients." Here indeed was Heaven-sent aid.

"Ah, my old and unesteemed friend, 'Danny the Dip,'" he murmured joyfully to himself. "On the look-out for some place where they've been obliging enough to forget to put the padlock on the back door! Pull up!" he ordered sharply, and in an instant he was out of the cab and into the blackness of the alley. A moment later he had dropped a hand upon the shoulder of the predatory figure. "Come on, Daniel," he advised sweetly. "It's a fair cop!"

Mr. Daniel Regan knew that voice as well—indeed, much better nowadays—as he knew the tones of his own mother.

"I've done nuttin', Inspector," he whined. "I was just looking about for a place to doss. I'm right on the floor!"

"It's a crime to be broke, Dan, one of the worst of the lot!" the inspector informed him. "So I'm afraid you can't get out of it that way. But," he added as he propelled the slight figure back towards Oxford Street, "I might overlook it this time if you were in the mind to do a little job for me."

"I'll do anythink, Inspector!" he was promptly informed. "I don' want to go 'inside' again—not just yet. The bloke at Marlborough Street told me that next time I come up he'd give me a 'twicer' and I ain't done a thing! 'Onest t' Gawd, I ain't! What is it y'r wantin' done, sir?"

"You see that gentleman over there?" McCarthy asked, pointing in the direction of the figure now well ahead of them. "You can't, I know, but he's there just the same."

"If he's there I'll pick him up, sir. Y' don't want to worry about that. I'll follow the sound of 'is feet. I can 'ear a cat in the dark—I got to at my game."

"I want him 'tailed' until he's treed for the night, Daniel, and I want the job done properly, and not just chucked the minute he goes inside any building out of which he may emerge again five minutes later, when he thinks he's got shut of you. And unless I'm much mistaken, you're following a very tricky gentleman, one who'll give you the slip the first chance you let him have. Now, you do this job for me and bring it off successfully, and bring me your report or, better still, send it to me over the telephone early to-morrow morning and I'll not only forgive your sins, past and present, but you'll be on ten bob as well. Maybe a quid if you make a *real* job of it," he added hearteningly.

"Could I 'ave a couple of bob to go on with, Inspector?" "Danny the Dip" pleaded hollowly. "Jest t' git a cup of cawfee if there's the chance while I'm on the job? I'm that 'ungry that me blasted guts seems to be 'angin' down about me knees, it's that sinkin'."

From the squad-car driver McCarthy borrowed shillings which he presented to the owner of the empty internals who grabbed at it avidly; the ravenous look in his eyes showed McCarthy that the tricky "Danny the Dip" was pulling no "spiel," but was indeed "on the floor."

"You know the 'phone number?" he shot quickly as the hungry one started off upon the trail of the solitary figure lost somewhere upon the other side of the road. "My own, I mean?"

"I don't think I do, Inspector. I know the Yard's."

McCarthy gave him his own 'phone number quickly, then "Danny the Dip" melted out of all sight into the blackness. McCarthy heaved a sigh as he climbed back into the car and ordered the driver to nip back into the square by way of Soho Street.

"And there goes a quid of my hard-earned stipend! And what the blazes for is more than I could tell you," he added ruefully.

"Well, there's one thing, sir, you won't have to cough up if he doesn't bring you something worth while," the driver consoled.

"I won't *have* to," McCarthy agreed, "but I know dashed well that I will! That's the sort of soft-hearted goat I am. You see," he concluded softly, "I've known what it is to be on the floor, and hungry, myself."

When the inspector returned to Soho Square he found it virtually cleared of the crowd; the autocratic, not to say high-handed, methods of the superintendent, plus the avoir-dupois of another dozen or so uniformed men had speedily convinced the gaping lot that the sooner they were out of the way the better for them.

In the case of those whom McCarthy had noted as persons engaged in pursuits which were, to say the least, dubious, one glance at them from Superintendent Burman's cold, grey eyes was plenty. They dived off towards whatever holes they inhabited, before he might decide that he wanted to put them through the hoop about something or other; probably something long since past, and for their part, almost forgotten. The verdict of predatory Soho upon Superintendent Burman was that he never seemed to forget anything; you never could tell with him.

Even the audience at the upper windows had apparently decided that nothing further of interest was going to happen that night. All he could dimly see in what was left of the fire-glow when he stepped out of the squad-car, was half a dozen or so of the more determined stickers at the farther corners of the square, the superintendent (fuming at being held up waiting for his car), the chief inspector, the sergeant and a couple of men who were to remain on duty at the spot during the night.

"You've been a devil of a long time, Mac," the superintendent growled. "What have you been up to?"

"Not so long as I expected to be," McCarthy returned equably and taking no notice whatever of the rather peevishly uttered, but quite justified question. He had long since discovered that the more you dodged the "Sooper's" questions, the less you were likely to be asked.

"I don't see that there's anything much that you can do here before daylight," Burman went on. "These two men will stay on duty all night to see that nothing's interfered with. It's an extraordinary thing to me how the body was disposed of in the time they had between that scream being heard and the police getting here."

"It certainly is extraordinary," McCarthy agreed. "I and the constable on beat must have been on the scene within two minutes of it—we made a dead-heat of it. Which is pretty fast work when you consider the black-out and that I was about to step into bed when it rang out. And as far as doing anything further here to-night, or, rather, this morning, goes, I agree with you that there isn't much possible. Still, I'll just take a look round to make sure. In any case I'll be here long before any of the occupiers of these offices show up, and, incidentally, a good looking-over them won't do any harm. By the way," he added quickly to the sergeant, "has anyone been put on the back entrance to this place?"

"I saw to that, sir," that competent officer told him. "There's a man there with orders to stick tight to his job till relieved."

"That's the stuff," McCarthy commended. "You can't beat the C. Division for knowing their job—and doing it!"

"Well, I'll be off," the superintendent said. "Let the C.I. have a report as soon as you've got anything tangible. Good night."

"There ye are, Sergeant," McCarthy said with a whimsical shake of his head as the car whirled his superior officers out of the square. "Let the chief-inspector know as soon as you've found anything tangible in a case where there's not even absolute certainty that there's been a murder committed! In other words dig out something definite, which there doesn't appear to be, let me know anything helpful and I'll give ye my kind advice as to how to proceed further! Sufferin' cats! Be thankful that you're in uniform and haven't got to pick up the jobs your superiors don't fancy, *and* can get to bed when your own work is done. We'll just take a look-see at your chap at the back. How do you get to it?"

The sergeant pointed out a narrow alley a little farther down which evidently led to another, running parallel with that side of the square, and used by dustmen and other social servitors. As they passed through it, by the light of the sergeant's torch McCarthy saw that a high wall ran along upon the side that the old house was situated. This, at the converging alley, gave place to a much lower one.

"Where the devil's Harper?" the sergeant muttered angrily. "He should have heard our steps and been out to see who it was, and dam' quick at that, in a business like this."

The same thought had also occurred to McCarthy. "We've moved very quietly, Sergeant," he reminded that irate officer. "It's just possible that the sound hasn't penetrated these thick walls?" he suggested.

"He'd no right to be behind the walls. My orders were to watch the gate and nowhere else," the other snapped. "He's not a 'rookie' who doesn't understand orders when they're given to him. He'll hear something from me that'll penetrate his thick skull," the sergeant growled. "I particularly cautioned him to be on the alert for anything." Taking his torch he flashed it along the alley, where its beam came to rest upon the figure of the constable leaning against the gate-post and, to judge by his attitude, fast asleep!

"Well, I'll be———!" he gasped. "*Asleep!* I'll finish him for this!"

He hurried along towards the unmoving figure.

"What the hell is this, Harper," he hissed. "You're for it, for this! I'll break you…"

"Steady!" McCarthy said in a quiet voice. "I doubt if you or anyone else will ever break him, Sergeant. Look at his face; he's not asleep. He's *dead!*"

Chapter VI

The Inside of the House

To say that Detective Inspector McCarthy was galvanized out of his usual imperturbable *sangfroid* by this ghastly discovery was to underestimate completely the extent of that officer's emotions, when he fully realized the situation. It needed but a moment's examination by the light of the sergeant's torch to settle definitely that the unfortunate constable had been in no way remiss in carrying out his duties. Far from it, he had undoubtedly been stabbed to an instantaneous death by someone who must have crept with absolute noiselessness up behind him, and, apparently, from the rear door of the house. Indeed, had Constable Harper not had his whole mind concentrated upon the alley he had been specifically instructed to watch, the likelihood was that he would have caught some sound of the killer creeping up behind him.

One of the extraordinary things about it was that he had not gone down when the blade had penetrated his heart, as undoubtedly it had instantly, but, in some strange way, not at once apparent, the whole weight of his bulk must have come to rest fairly against the solid gatepost, which had supported it in an upright position.

Of the method of his killing there could be no argument whatever; the first glance at his back showed that beyond any question of doubt. There was a small triangular-shaped hole in his broad back, immediately at the rear of his heart, from which the blood was still welling, slowly, and thickly. He must have died with scarcely the quiver of a muscle, and his face, now gone the grey of death, showed not the slightest distortion of pain.

A groan broke from McCarthy's lips.

"What a cursed fool I was not to have realized the probability of that front door having been used as a getaway," he said. "But its very appearance made me positive in my own mind that it hadn't been. My first act should have been to have sent a couple of men to stand guard over the rear door and make sure of anyone who might've taken cover inside the house. If I'd done that," he went on mournfully, "this poor fellow would have been alive now."

"It almost looks," the sergeant said, in little more than a whisper, "as though the body of the murdered person must've been dragged inside after all. I couldn't see any other way that they could have got rid of it in the time they had."

"It certainly does," McCarthy admitted.

Pulling his automatic from his pocket and releasing the safety-catch, he then turned the torch upon the back door. It was partly open.

"Adding two and two together, there's not much doubt as to how the killer escaped," he muttered. "Just how long is it since you sent this poor fella round here, Sergeant?"

"Not a minute after you went off in the squad-car, sir," the sergeant informed him. "I knew that that was what you'd have done yourself if—if you hadn't had something else on your mind just at the moment."

"That damned hunch of mine to follow that fellow," McCarthy groaned. "In that case, Sergeant," he went on, "whoever killed Harper must've left the house, committed the deed and walked quietly out through that alley and into Soho Square, while Superintendent Burman, the chief inspector and yourself were colloguing at the front door. Harper's not been dead many minutes—his hands are not really cold yet."

"It must've been about that time," the sergeant agreed.

One thought flashed across McCarthy's mind instantly: that whoever had done this second killing, it most certainly could not have been the man with the ice-blue eyes. Indeed, why he should be connected with the business in any shape or form was something the inspector would have been at a big loss to explain to anyone. However, he most certainly had not been connected with this ghastly second portion of it.

"We'll have to go through the whole place, Sergeant," he said. "Though I'm afraid we'll only draw blank."

"There's a mighty big likelihood that we'll find the other body somewhere at the back of that front door," the sergeant said stubbornly. "At least, I think there is."

"You're probably right," McCarthy admitted, a trifle wearily. "I was wrong about the door having been opened; I'm probably wrong about that as well."

He led the way across a small paved yard to that partly-opened door, threw it right back and turned the torch into it. Owing to its conformation, it was impossible to see right through to the front door, despite its width, for the staircase which led from the hall was a particularly wide and magnificently carved one, as was also that portion of it which continued down into a basement. Across the hall there were also two pillars supporting arches which also helped to break the view.

"You'll notice, sir," the sergeant mentioned as they stepped into the rear part of the hall, "that this back door has a spring lock."

"So much the better," McCarthy said. "Shut it after you. If there's anyone hidden in the basement, by any chance, they'll have a bit of a job to slip us. In any case we'll search that first—after we've made sure that there is, or is not, as it may be, a body in the hall."

Turning his torch to the floor, his eyes searching for blood spots upon the old and worn linoleum, the inspector led the way towards the extremely wide front door. No sign was there to be seen of anything out of the ordinary, and certainly nothing to suggest that the victim of whatever tragedy might have occurred outside, had been brought into the actual premises, themselves. Not one drop of blood was there to be seen, except in one place: on the outer fringe of the sunken doormat, which ran right across, and slightly under the door itself. That had evidently trickled down from the outer side of the door, and worked its way underneath.

"Well," McCarthy asked quietly, "are you satisfied now about the body being brought into the inside?"

In the light of the torch the sergeant stared helplessly at the wide door mat, and that portion of the hall which lay between it and the stairs. The evidence of his own eyes was irrefutable; most certainly nothing, or no one, bleeding as they must have been doing, had been brought through that door.

"There we are, Sergeant," McCarthy said, but in no cock-sure way, "let it be a lesson to ye never to be certain of anything, where murder is concerned. I was positive in my own mind that the door had never been opened, though why I was is more than I could tell you at the moment. But I was, and I was wrong. You were fairly sure that the body had been got away through it; you, too, were wrong. You can see for yourself how utterly impossible it would have been to do it without leaving, at least, a bloodstain or some tell-tale mark or other."

He next gave his attention to the huge, old-fashioned box lock of the door; from the size of it and its cumbersomeness, generally, it might well have been the original article, fitted when the house had been built. Its key must have been an enormous one, but, although it was locked, there was no sign of it. The door was also secured by two large iron bolts, top and bottom, both of which were shot. There was a spring lock set in above the old one.

"Nice chance we'd have had of breaking in here," the inspector commented.

"Not much, and that's a fact," the sergeant agreed, "we'd have had to have made entry by one of the windows. Though, of course," he corrected himself, "there'd be the door from that area where you found the knife and the handkerchief."

"We'd have found it bolted quite as securely as this one, I don't doubt," McCarthy said. "Anyhow, as we're here you'd better bawl through the keyhole to the man on duty outside, and get him to send for the divisional-surgeon and the ambulance to remove Harper's body to the mortuary. He'd better request your inspector to send some more men here at the same time. Tell him to instruct them to come to the back door with as little fuss as possible—and, under no circumstances, are any of them—*any* of them, mark y'—to so much as set foot inside that back gate until I've had a chance to go over the ground by daylight. And, moreover," he added quickly as the sergeant was stooping to poke open the shield of a fairly large letter-slit to use it for transmitting his instructions, "for the love of Mike tell him to keep his hands off the door, and be careful not to let anyone else touch it. That may also have something to tell when I've a chance to get at it in daylight."

These instructions being faithfully, indeed almost belligerently, bawled through the keyhole to the man outside, the sergeant turned again to McCarthy.

"What next, sir?" he asked.

The inspector was giving his attention to the entirely modern Yale lock set in the upper part of the door.

"That was the mode of entrance, of course," he remarked. "The big lock, in all probability, is not used at all—a clumsy contraption, and quite out of date. Though, of course," he added, "there's just a chance that it may be locked as a sort of additional safeguard last thing in the evening by the charladies when they depart. They'd probably exit by that back door, and the boy you spoke of come in by the same way."

But the sergeant shook his head.

"No, sir," he said, very positively, "both the charwomen leave by the front door because I've seen them, and I've also seen the lad let himself in by the front door in the morning."

"Hm," McCarthy uttered musingly. "In that case, it isn't possible for this big lock and those bolts to be used at all. So the situation, on the face of it, looks to be this. If the man who committed the outside crime came through this way, he must have let himself in by a latchkey, then turned the key in the big lock, and shot the bolts. The reason for that is obvious: to gain time should the police, arriving hurriedly on top of that scream, attempt to force entrance here. Finding that they did not, and that he had time to take things calmly, he stayed quietly where he was, until he thought it safe to venture out and make a getaway by the back door and through that alley.

"The possibilities are that there was another reason that made him wait for a bit before venturing forth. Just at that time the glare from the fire was at its height and he probably thought he'd be wiser to hang back for a bit in case someone spotted him in the glare. When at last he *did* take a chance it was to discover Harper on duty at the back gate. To get out he had to finish him, once and for all; a business that wouldn't be over difficult to an expert knife-man, as the evidence seems to show that this fellow was. After that it would be comparatively easy to get well away from this place, or even mingle with the crowd and watch events."

"But—but Harper hadn't been dead more than two or three minutes before we found him," the sergeant objected.

"Thereabouts," McCarthy said, "but a man in a desperate hurry can travel a divil of a long way in that time. It's quite on the cards that he scaled the fence on the other side of the alley, and made off that way."

"That's possible," the sergeant said, casting his mental eye over the neighbourhood. "He could have got out and into Chapel Street if he knew his ground."

"I think we can take it for granted that he did that," McCarthy said. "We'll take a look about the place."

The rooms upon the first floor were all locked, as McCarthy expected to find; the one upon the immediate right-hand side upon entering the front door seemed to be the office of whatever management there was about the place. That, too, was locked.

"And I expect that we'll find them all the same right up to the attics," McCarthy said. "If there is such a thing as a board where duplicate keys to the offices are kept, or even a master key, it will be in that office, and unless we're going to break in every door in the place, which I don't propose doing, we can't get very much farther, as far as the offices are concerned. Unfortunately," he added, a twinkle in his eye, "I haven't my little pick-lock with me."

"We might break into this office and see if there's a master key," the sergeant said, though dubiously.

"Break into a place without a properly issued warrant," McCarthy said severely. "I am surprised at you, Sergeant! And, at that, a place which doesn't show one exterior sign that a crime's been committed in it. D'ye see any spots of blood, or bullet holes through the door or anything else to justify you taking such an action?"

"No, sir," the sergeant replied sheepishly.

McCarthy shook his head, as though grieved beyond measure at even the thought of such an outrage.

"You want to watch your step, Sergeant," he said warningly. "One or two of those little larks, and you'll be getting as bad a name as myself with the higher-ups. We'll try the basement; I don't suppose that will be locked up like a bank vault."

Descending the stairs, they came upon a set of rooms which must in bygone days have composed the kitchen and other domestic offices of the old house. By the look of them they must have been gloomy holes at the best of times, and at the present moment looked like so many dungeons. The doors were all flung wide open and it needed little more than a cursory glance to show that they were filled with useless lumber of all sorts, buried in the dust of years. In McCarthy's opinion they certainly had nothing to tell but, before turning upstairs again, he gave the floorings by the doors a careful examination; they too were so thickly covered with dust that a recent footprint would have stood out as plainly as if stencilled.

"There's no one entered any of these rooms to-night, Sergeant," he said didactically.

At that moment a police whistle sounded at the rear of the house—the signal arranged by the sergeant to notify them on the arrival of the divisional-surgeon and the ambulance.

"That's them," the sergeant said with complete certitude, and an equally complete lack of grammar.

McCarthy made a dart up the stairs, taking three at a time.

"Quick with that back-door key," he snapped, "before they start rubbing out every footprint between the door and the back gate with their Number Ten's! And when you go out," he added, "watch that you step well to one side of the path clear of any possible spoor."

One glance the divisional-surgeon gave at that portion of the murdered Harper's back which was lit by the torch.

"I don't know what the devil I'm supposed to do here," he was beginning, when McCarthy interrupted him.

"Now, Doctor, darlin', don't start bellyaching the minute you get here," he said, a whimsical note in his voice. "'Tis the prerogative of the medical profession called from their warm, downy beds I know, but there's quite a point or two that you can put me right on for a start."

"Damme if I see what they are," the slightly mollified medico said, "as I understand it, you found the man within a few minutes of his murder, so you know the time of death as well as I do. That he's been stabbed is as plain as a pike-staff—even a C.I.D. man could see that."

"Ah," McCarthy said, "but what with, Doctor? That's the point."

"What do you think it would be with—a safety razor blade?"

"If you'll take a *look* and not a cursory glance at what's to be seen of that wound," McCarthy went on, taking no notice of the gibe, "ye'll notice that it's three-cornered, that shows most definitely in the cut in the heavy cloth of the tunic."

"I can see that," the medical man said, still grumpily. "What about it?"

"I'd be glad to know just what class of weapon, in your opinion, the poor fella was killed with."

From his pocket the doctor took a magnifying glass and made a closer inspection of the wound.

"A three-edged dagger, undoubtedly," he said positively. "That's clear enough. I should say that it carried a well-sharpened point which punctured the heart and caused death instantly."

From the pocket of his dressing-gown, McCarthy produced carefully the dagger he had found in the front of the house.

"Could this be the weapon, Doc?" he asked quietly.

The medical man took the stiletto gingerly by the haft and examined it. "It could be," he pronounced, "and I should be inclined to say it is."

McCarthy shook his head. "Taking events chronologically as they happened, Doctor, it couldn't very well be the actual weapon," he said. "I found this a good half an hour, approximately, before Harper, here, was stabbed."

"Then if not that particular weapon, he was killed with one as like it as possible," the doctor said. "By the way, would you like me to take a test from the blood on that weapon?"

"That's an idea," the inspector said. "I'll have it finger-printed and sent on to you right away. There's no need to keep you here any longer, Doctor. Get the body away to the mortuary as soon as you're ready. Will you do the P.M. to-night—or rather this morning?"

"I may as well," the medical gentleman growled. "Get it done with, and if I've any luck I may get a bit of breakfast in peace, even if I can't get any sleep."

"Well, Sergeant, I think I'm about through here for to-night," McCarthy said, as they watched the rear light of the ambulance, followed by the divisional-surgeon's two-seater, disappear out of the alley. Put a couple of men on here, back and front, and by that I mean two at each point, with instructions not to pass the gate at this point or touch the front door at the other. I'll be here first thing in the morning to meet this youth that opens up. And when I say a couple of men—you'll know I'll mean by that: that I don't want any further repetition of this wicked Harper business."

"You think there's any possibility of that, Inspector?" the sergeant asked quickly.

"I'm not chancing it," McCarthy said.

"It's a mystery to me," the sergeant murmured reflectively, as they made their way along the alley back to Soho Square.

"What became of that body—the one that was hacked up in the front, I mean? I suppose," he added, a trifle maliciously, "that you're satisfied in your mind that it was a human that was carved up there, and not some foul brute carving up a dog, or something of that sort."

"Definitely," McCarthy said imperturbably. "I could have told you then that it was a human who'd been killed, and, moreover, that he, or she, had had her jugular vein and probably other main arteries severed."

"Then why," the sergeant was beginning, when McCarthy went on.

"All I pointed out to you, Sergeant, was that there was no actual, visual *evidence* that it was a murder, and, come to that, there's no more now. But a severed human jugular, or at any rate a main artery was the one thing which could account, not only for the quantity of blood there was, but the way it was splashed about. In that connection it's on one of the razor-like edges of that stiletto in which the blood is clotted thickest and not the point, as it would have been had it been a clean stab, such as Harper was killed with.

"That showed that the victim was slashed viciously, which again suggests hatred, or possibly revenge, as a motive, which certainly wasn't so in Harper's case. And for the last thing, the air simply reeked of perfume when I got there, and I'd say an expensive one at that. It hadn't had time then to evaporate. It isn't the usual custom of men, even foreigners of the dandified class, to use perfume these days."

"I knew that scream came from a woman," the sergeant said with conviction.

"I think I pointed out to you once before to-night, that it might possibly prove to be the woman who was the killer," the inspector said dryly. "Though I'm bound to say that it's not over likely. Well," he said, "we've got that something 'tangible' that the 'Sooper' wanted, if it's only concerning the murder of poor Harper. But all the same it isn't all wasted work. Now that we know that the front door was used we've got something definite to work on, and a very useful 'something' at that."

"I don't just see," the sergeant was commencing, when McCarthy interrupted.

"We know that whoever escaped out of the square through that door, had a latch-key which admitted them to the place. That narrows things down to a comparatively small circle of people. According to all the rules, Sergeant, that fact ought to put someone in the dock on the capital charge, sooner or later."

"It should *that*," the sergeant admitted readily. "I didn't think of that for the minute, Inspector."

"But the unfortunate thing about murder, Sergeant," McCarthy pursued in that whimsical tone of his, "is that it is never committed according to any rules. The thing that you're positive is going to happen is generally the last thing that does. If it turns out any different in this case, then it'll be the exception which proves the rule."

Chapter VII

"Danny the Dip" Turns Up

Inspector McCarthy, minus the sergeant's torch, began to creep his way back in the direction of his lodgings. Any helpful light that might have come from the glowing embers of the fire had been long since blotted out by the exertions of the fire brigade. He had not proceeded very far when he thudded against some extremely solid human object who, upon mutual investigation, turned out to be C. 1285, back again upon his beat.

As the constable was in possession of a torch, which, by the way, Regulations did not permit him to use except in a moment of crisis, the inspector borrowed it from him, and the two proceeded side by side towards the middle of Greek Street until the inspector's way obliged him to turn out of that thoroughfare.

"Strange case that to-night, sir," C. 1285 ventured, after a moment.

"Extraordinary," McCarthy answered affably. "'Tis jobs like that that keep us up on our toes, and, incidentally"—he stifled a yawn—"out of our beds."

"I've managed to discover that there was one vehicle went out of Soho Square, and must have come through it just about the time of that scream," the constable went on. "That is," he added dubiously, "if you could call it a vehicle."

"What was that?" McCarthy asked quickly.

"Old Joe Anselmi's portable coffee-stall," the constable told him. "That's a regular job, though he generally gets it through the square with a couple of helpers about half-past eleven. But to-night, for some reason or other he was late, I suppose the two chaps who generally help him to push it to his stand didn't turn up and he must have waited till just before one, and then had to shove it himself—a bit of a job for an old man."

McCarthy nodded. He knew old Joe Anselmi well; had done so ever since he himself had been a lad knocking about the purlieus of Soho. A respectable hard-working old man, a rigid and devout Catholic, and one most certainly not likely to be connected with crime in any shape or form whatsoever.

"It certainly must have been a job for the old man to push a lumbering thing like that along by himself," he agreed. "And he turned out of the square just at that time you say? Which way did he go?"

"By Sutton Street into the Charing Cross Road," he was told. "His pitch, as I suppose you know, Inspector, is at a corner just a bit down Denman Street."

"I know," McCarthy said. A good many times when out upon a nocturnal prowl he had pulled up at the old man's stall for a cup of coffee and a chow about bygone days in Soho. Certainly that unwieldy portable place of business was not to be connected in any way with the crime in Soho Square.

Arrived at the corner at which he turned right to make his way through into Dean Street, while the constable's beat took him to the left towards Frith Street, they parted company.

"Look in to my place for the torch and a drink in the morning," he said. "The kind of luck I'm having to-night I'd have broken my neck without the loan of it long before this. Good night."

Inside his own room he once again divested himself of his dressing-gown and prepared to turn in; he would have to be out bright and early in the morning to get to the scene of the crime before anyone connected with that queer lot of offices arrived there. For a moment it was in his mind to give Bill Haynes a ring, but he decided against it. Knowing the Assistant Commissioner's enthusiasm where sticky crimes of the sort just committed were concerned, he would be probably kept up the greater part of what little time remained to him for sleep jawing the whole thing over again.

He seemed to have been asleep but five minutes when the telephone at his bedside rang out at an alarming rate. Starting up he switched on his light, glanced at his wrist-watch to discover that it was five o'clock, then lifted the receiver.

"What is it *now?*" he demanded, a not unnatural tartness in his voice.

He was informed that he was being called by the "S" Division station at Golders Green, and that the inspector in charge was speaking.

"Golders Green!" McCarthy echoed. "What in the name of Heaven does Golders Green want with me, Inspector?"

"There's a rather strange and ugly business happened at this end, Inspector," he was informed. "We wouldn't have troubled you but for the fact that there's a man named Regan concerned in it—Dan Regan, who we know to be a West End pickpocket."

"'Danny the Dip'!" McCarthy snapped. "What's the matter with him?"

"He's telling a story that takes a bit of believing, Inspector," the voice at the other end of the line went on. "He says that he was doing a certain job for you when he was knocked out in Park Lane. The next thing he knew when he came to was that he was wandering about on the Heath. He didn't know where he was, and had the idea that he was in Hyde Park. One of my men on beat found him wandering about near the Vale of Health, and brought him in. He's in an absolutely bemused state, and I'd say he has been given a shot of something or other. He hardly seems to know what he is talking about, but he sticks to the tale that he was doing a job for you."

"He's quite right there, Inspector," McCarthy said. "I left him in Oxford Street doing a bit of shadowing for me. Can't he give any explanation as to what has happened to him?"

"Nothing that seems to make sense," came the prompt answer. "And there's another side of it too: he's covered with blood; far more than the crack over the head he's undoubtedly had will account for."

"The poor divil has run into bad trouble somewhere or other," McCarthy said ruefully. "Too bad; too bad, entirely."

"There's something considerably worse than that which the constable discovered at the same time," the voice continued. "Not far from where Regan was found wandering about, he discovered the body of a woman who had been brutally murdered. Her throat had been cut until the head was nearly severed from the body, and she had other wounds as well."

"What's that!" McCarthy almost yelled into the phone. "Repeat that, Inspector!"

With the greatest possible succinctness the "S" Division officer did so.

"What type of woman did she seem to be and how long does your D.S. say she's been dead?" McCarthy got out all in one breath.

He was told that as far as could be judged by exteriors, the quality of her clothes, etc., etc., the murdered woman appeared, at any rate, to belong to the wealthy class. The body was clad in evening dress, covered by a coat which certainly had cost a considerable amount of money, and although no jewellery or anything else had been found upon her, there were distinct evidences that she had been in the habit of wearing rings, and the lobe of one ear was torn as though an ear-ring had been wrenched from it. The divisional-surgeon had been called, and, though only making a short and cursory examination, had given it as his opinion that she had been murdered somewhere in the region of midnight or perhaps a little later, but not more than an hour or so, in his opinion.

"Where is the body now?" McCarthy asked quickly.

He was told that it was at the local mortuary, but that the D.S. did not propose carrying out the post-mortem until the morning.

"Listen, Inspector," McCarthy said quickly. "Have the body transferred at once—*at once*, you understand me—to the mortuary here. I'll call up our divisional-surgeon and tell him to get there at once. I believe it to be the body of a person murdered in Soho Square somewhere about one o'clock to-night, and spirited away in some mysterious fashion. Now get that straight, like a good fella, as positive orders from H.Q."

"But," the local inspector was beginning, some objection obviously in his mind, when McCarthy interrupted.

"I'll have the orders sent direct to you from the Assistant Commissioner, within ten minutes, if that occurs to ye as the proper proceeding, Inspector," he said. "Come to think of it, perhaps it would be. Red tape can play the very divil with a man if he puts a foot wrong. Stand by for a call from the A.C. within a few minutes of my getting off the line, and at the same time send Regan in to the mortuary in the first vehicle you can grab hold of. Now get busy, time is the whole essence of this particular thing. S'long—and thanks for the call, though how you found my number is a mystery to me."

"Regan knew it," the inspector told him. "It was that that made us think there might be something in his yarn."

Ringing off, McCarthy promptly dialled the number of Sir William Haynes' Bloomsbury residence, and a moment later had him on the line. Quickly he poured into that staggered gentleman's ear a brief résumé of what had happened since they had parted, and requested the prompt transference of the body from Golders Green to the West End.

"Golders Green is naturally standing on a bit of etiquette, Bill," he concluded, "but a word from you direct will put that right, and when you've done that ye might give our sawbones a personal tinkle to pull up his socks and get himself to the mortuary without any undue delay. He was bellyachin' at being lugged to Soho Square to view poor Harper's body, and what he'll have to say if I have him routed out again will be unfit for publication. His howls will go up to the high heaven! He's not a bad old stick and knows his job inside out, but he does like his bed. So do I," he added whimsically, "and, if you remember, I promised myself a full issue of it to-night, and here's the result. Get busy, Bill—the chap at Golders Green is hanging on for your O.K."

"Would you care for me to get dressed and slip along to the mortuary, Mac?" Sir William asked eagerly.

"Very far from it," his friend answered promptly and succinctly. "Definitely, *no!* To start with," he added in more mollifying tones, "you'd probably break your neck on the road there, Bill, and as I told you once before to-night, what Scotland Yard would do without you is more than I, or anyone else, could say. The blow would be shattering."

Before Sir William could reply to these somewhat invidious remarks, McCarthy rang off, and made a dive for his clothes.

Five minutes later saw him out in the street again, but this time fully garbed and torched. This Soho Square murder was beginning to open up in an unusually strange manner, but perhaps the queerest part of it to the inspector, and the angle of it he was most interested in at the moment, was what had happened to "Danny the Dip" after he had left him in Oxford Street on the heels of the man with those unnatural-looking ice-blue eyes.

Chapter VIII

The Inspector Sustains a Shock!

The body which McCarthy found stretched out fully dressed upon a slab in the mortuary when, at last, he managed to make his way to that charnel house, undoubtedly bore out the description given to it by the inspector at Golders Green as suggesting that of a woman of a certain social position and, certainly, affluent circumstances.

He found it already in charge of the divisional-surgeon who, marvellous to relate, was accepting this most recent call upon him quite cheerfully; indeed, seemed rather bucked about it than otherwise. The Assistant Commissioner, he thought, must have buttered the medical gentleman well and truly when he rang him, to have this effect upon his usually anything but philosophic nature.

A glance into the little office room wherein the mortuary-keeper kept the belongings, carefully parcelled and tabulated, of those unfortunate enough to be brought into this gloomy bourne showed him that "Danny the Dip" had been forwarded on along with the cadaver, and was seated in a chair looking very much as though he were but half awake from a heavy dope sleep. Indeed, he stared at the inspector as though he scarcely recognized him.

"Can you give that chap a shot of anything that will fully awaken his faculties, Doc?" he asked quietly.

"I can," the medical man answered with a doubtful glance at the dishevelled-looking, bloodstained figure of the pickpocket. "But if you want to get anything out of him immediately, I'd suggest a hot, strong cup of tea will have quicker results. He's had an injection of one of the barbituary drugs by the look of him. Morphine or heroin, I'd say."

McCarthy glanced at the mortuary-keeper. "Can you manage it, do y' think?"

That worthy nodded affirmatively. There were not many for whom he would have put himself to any trouble at that hour of the morning, but Inspector McCarthy was an especial favourite of his. The D.S. could have asked for it till his tongue withered without moving the burly official.

"'Tis aisy, Inspector," he said, in his strong Hibernian brogue. "I'll stick a kittle on me little oil stove." He bent a huge head towards the inspector and cast a glance back towards the vacant-looking Regan. "Have ye noticed th' state his clothes are in?" he whispered. "'Tis blood he is fr'm head to foot. He never got it from that dab on the nut, and he doesn't seem to be hurrted anny other place."

"So the inspector at Golders Green informed me," McCarthy responded, with a worried look towards his late assistant. "We'll go into that later, when he's in better shape. Load him up with tea, hot and strong."

"I'll pour a pint of it into him, boilin', before he's five minutes older," the mortuary-keeper assured him. "An' if that don't do the thrick, I'll pour another."

With this assurance McCarthy turned towards the female body upon the slab.

That she had been a handsome and certainly perfectly gowned woman but a few short hours ago there was no doubt, nor had the inspector at Golders Green been far out when he had said that the coat which covered a high fronted—and doubtless bare-backed—evening gown had cost a considerable amount of money. It was ermine and cut in the very latest mode, but the collar and front of the garment were literally steeped in blood from the ghastly throat wound which had most certainly brought about her death.

As the inspector had said, her head had been nearly severed from her body—the work of some absolutely fiendish butcher. The very savagery of the crime explained at once to McCarthy that wallow of blood upon the door, the outer steps and even the railings. The coat also explained by the very thickness of its fur the means by which the body had been got away without leaving any traces beyond those mentioned: the whole head and shoulders had been wrapped in it, thus preventing any seepage of the tell-tale fluid. It was equally possible that the vehicle, whatever it might have been, used to transport the cadaver from the square would be found equally free from bloodstains when it might eventually be picked up—if ever.

"You're quite sure it's the body in the Soho business, Mac?" the divisional-surgeon asked.

"Quite," McCarthy answered positively. "Unless," he amended, "two women were murdered in London to-night at about the same time and in the same manner, and both used the same perfume to a degree rather more than most women to-day are in the habit of doing. I got it strongly outside the Soho Square house and there's no mistaking it for anything but the same that this unfortunate creature has been using."

The doctor nodded. "I get it myself," he said. "It's queer."

It was on the tip of McCarthy's tongue to ask what was queer about it, but as he did not want to listen to any discourse upon perfumes, generally, and this particular one specifically he withheld the question and turned again to his examination. Everything she wore, shoes, stockings and lingerie all carried the hallmark of expensiveness and quality. There were, as he had been informed by Golders Green, definite signs upon the fingers that she had worn rings upon each hand, and the mark was plainly to be seen where one ear-ring, at least, had been ruthlessly torn from the right ear-lobe. As neither of the ears had been pierced they must have been screw or clip fastenings, and that they had been taken at all seemed to argue that they must have been of considerable value. In the inside of the coat, which now lay wide open and overhanging the slab upon one side, there was a pocket into which he thrust his hand and brought out a solid gold cigarette-case which, however, carried no monogram or other possible means of identification; nor, that he could see upon a cursory examination, were there any markings on the underclothes.

He gave some little time to a study of the face itself, upon which the grey pallor of death seemed to show strangely through the heavy coating of make-up the woman wore. He decided that it was of a definitely Continental type, and not English; Teutonic, he would have said, with extraordinarily strong features for one of her sex.

"What nationality would you put her down as being, Doc?" he asked.

"German," the D.S. answered unhesitatingly. "A perfect Teutonic cast of features; no doubt about that in my mind. Is that the only thing you notice about it, Mac?" he continued, a note in his voice which made the inspector glance at him quickly.

"What else is there to see?" McCarthy questioned. "Besides that she was a woman of distinction in her early, or mid-thirties, I'd say, and of a particularly strong cast of features, what is there to see?"

"A devil of a lot that will surprise you," the medico answered. "That is," he amended, "if anything can."

"It can't," McCarthy assured him equably, "but I'll listen, just the same."

"Well, if this doesn't, I'll eat my hat," the surgeon said tersely. "Your woman, McCarthy, happens to be a man!"

It was useless for the inspector to even try to hide the complete and utter surprise which filled him. His eyes bulged and his jaw dropped.

"Well, I'll—I'll go to hell!" he gasped. "You're not codding, I suppose?" he asked quickly.

"If you think I enjoy being lugged out of bed at this hour of the morning so much that I start codding people, you're very much mistaken," the medico growled. "Your lady, I repeat, is a man. To satisfy yourself just run your hand upwards under the chin. If there aren't bristles enough under the make-up to set your mind at rest upon that point, then you take a deuce of a lot of satisfying."

McCarthy gingerly did as he was told, to find, beyond any question of doubt, that under his hand was unquestionably the bristles of a strong beard, but so skilfully covered by the make-up that, in the ordinary way, they were absolutely undetectable.

"A common enough type in Germany nowadays," the D.S. commented. "The last time I was in Berlin the lounges of the Hotel Adlon, and similar places, were full of them. The pure Aryan," he continued sarcastically, "seems to have a very definite leaning in that direction. As far as the bristles go, he probably shaves two or three times a day; had he been alive and he'd done that this morning, we wouldn't have found a trace of them. The D.S. at Golders Green must have taken a very cursory glance at him—the teeth alone ought to have told him the truth, though I'll admit that they are exceptionally small."

"They didn't me," McCarthy said ruefully.

"Which is only proof, if you need any, that you don't know as much as you think you do, Mac," the surgeon returned dryly.

"But what the divil is he got up in this way, here in England, for?" McCarthy questioned, though more to himself than anyone else.

The D.S. shrugged his shoulders. "That's *your* job to find out. Personally, I'd say it was a case of espionage in some form or other. There are any amount of them here among the 'refugees' and 'anti-Nazis.' We're the dam'dest fools on earth when it comes to that sort of thing."

"You're telling *me!*" McCarthy exclaimed. "You want to hear the Special Branch men on that."

"I don't," the other said shortly. "I've got plenty of grouses of my own, without having to listen to theirs. However, you're aware now that it's the murder of a man you're investigating, and not a woman. Though," he amended, "and speak with all caution, I'd say that he was in the habit of wearing female clothes habitually, if I make myself clear."

McCarthy nodded. "You mean that I'm investigating the case of the murder of a man who isn't known in the country as a man at all, but as a woman?"

"That's it. And now, I'll thank you to clear out and let me get on with my job. Unless," he added, with a jerk of his head towards another still figure stretched out upon a slab at the other end of the chill room, "there's anything you want to know about the murdered constable. I made a thorough examination of his wound, and I've come to the conclusion that it's more than likely that he was stabbed with an exact counterpart of that weapon you showed me. The sooner you can let me have it, the better, and I'll get on with the blood test you wanted."

"I'll give the 'dabs' artist's a ring and hustle them up," McCarthy promised. He was turning away towards the office, in which "Danny the Dip" was now being regaled with a huge mug of tea, which, from the steam arising from it, must have been well-nigh scalding, when something else crossed his mind. "Then that hair," he said, with a nod towards the cadaver stretched out before them, "must be a wig."

"Of course; no man living could ever train his hair to grow that way, even though it is on the short side."

Lifting the head, the D.S. unfastened several almost invisible hairpins, and drew an amazingly perfect wig of dark brown hair, very slightly touched with grey, from it. "Wonderful piece of real-hair work," he commented. "Quite the best I've ever come across, must have been made by an artist in that line. Practically undetectable in the ordinary way."

Holding out his hand for the wig, McCarthy took it, and examined it thoroughly. Among the odds and ends of miscellaneous information he had picked up from theatrical friends, was the fact that first-class wig-makers invariably stitched a tab with their name and the date of making, and very often the name of the person the wig was made for, upon the inside webbing on which the hair was threaded. If by any lucky chance it should be so in this case—and certainly the magnificent wig the "woman" had worn could only have been the work of a first-class maker—then here might be a direct clue which might, eventually, lead to the identity of the murdered man. Surely enough upon one corner of the tapes, which held the springs which formed the foundation of the wig, he came across a small printed tab bearing the inscription, "Heinrich, London." But he could find no date or anything else that would give the slightest clue as to who the wig had been made for.

"I'll want this for a bit," he said to the attendant. "Parcel it up, and I'll sign for it. How's Regan going on?"

"Foine," he was told. "The tay done 'im all the good in the world, like the D.S. said it would. But there's one thing, Inspector, ye'll need get him an overcoat of some sort or other before ye can take 'im out of this. If he goes out on the street the way he is, with the blood dried all over him, he'll be pinched for murder before he gets a hundred yards, even with you with him."

A glance into the office where Regan sat sipping at the scalding tea and pulling horrible faces in the process, satisfied McCarthy of the truth of the observation. "Find him something for the time being," he requested. "I'll take him home with me to hear his story, and return anything you can dig him up later in the day.

"How are you feeling now, Dan?" he asked, as he entered the office.

The pickpocket looked up at him through still half-vacant eyes.

"Bloody awful," he answered in a tone which left no doubt in McCarthy's mind as to the truth of his words. "They musta soaked me proper, Inspector, while they was at it," he continued, with a shake of his head. "Blimey, many's the time I been put down with bars an' bottles and coshes, but I never felt like this."

"They gave you something else, to make sure of you, Dan," McCarthy explained. "A shot of something that would keep you where they wanted you for as long as it suited them."

As he spoke his eyes were travelling over the thick, dark stains upon Regan's clothes. "You've no idea what happened to you after they knocked you out, Danny?" he inquired.

Regan shook his head. "After they dotted me, guv'nor, an' I seen a million stars, I dunno nothink. I 'spect I must've been dumped into a car, because it was out of one that they dived on me, and I couldn't 'ave got all the way to 'Ampstead any other way, like I must've done."

McCarthy nodded his agreement.

"No, Danny," he said, "it was a car, right enough. I'll take you home with me for a bit of breakfast, and hear your story up to that point there. The thing that's interesting me most at the moment, is where, and how, did you come by all this blood on your clothes. You certainly never got it from that crack on the skull."

Regan shook his head wearily. "Don't ask me, Inspector," he returned. "You know as much abaht that as I do."

Taking a small penknife from his pocket, McCarthy wiped the blade clean, then carefully scraped some of the glutinous, and still moist in parts, blood from Regan's coat. Spreading it carefully upon a sheet of white paper he got from the mortuary attendant, he took it back to the doctor and requested him to make a test with that of the man in female clothing.

"I've the idea, Doc," he said, "that the body of this man was already in the bottom of the car that Regan was pitched into, and the blood from this one will be found to be the same that he's covered with."

"Leave it here," the D.S. said brusquely. "I'll do the lot at the same time. And if there's anything else you can think up to keep me stuck at it here all day, don't hesitate to rush it along. My time is of no account whatever," he added sarcastically.

"I'll not forget," McCarthy said, with a grin, and, first seeing his battered assistant arrayed in an ancient rain-coat six sizes too big for him, led the way towards the door.

Taking a last glance back at the figure upon which the disgruntled doctor was now engaged in stripping of its misleading apparel, something struck him concerning it which, until that moment, had not.

The shaven head without the wig intensified tremendously the Teutonic caste of the dead man's face, even masked in make-up as it was. There, unquestionably, was your Prussian of the officer class. During his many visits to the Continent upon police business he had seen dozens who might have been blood brothers of the dead man. He had little doubt that, when the face was eventually cleaned off, the scars of student duelling affairs would be found bitten into it.

"Espionage, right enough," he murmured. "But in what connection, and who was sufficiently antagonistic to what you were up to, to make a slaughterhouse end of you, such as they have done?"

Chapter IX

The Inspector Gets Yet Another Shock

It was, McCarthy's watch told him, a little after seven o'clock when he left the mortuary, followed by Regan, still a little shaky upon his feet. Away to the east, light was beginning to disperse the gloom of the black-out, and for the first time the inspector was thankful for the resumption of normal time. Otherwise it would have meant another groping journey back to Dean Street; quite bad enough in those narrow thoroughfares, even with a torch.

They pushed along in silence, McCarthy feeling in no mood for talking after the recent major surprise discovery, and, apparently, Mr. Regan still less so—unless his particular silence was to be put down to an observance of the golden rule of speaking when he was spoken to. By the time they arrived in Regent Street it was quite daylight.

"We'll turn down as far as Glasshouse Street, Danny, and cut through to my crib that way," the inspector said suddenly. "It'll have to be a hasty breakfast, because I'm due in Soho Square before eight o'clock."

At Glasshouse Street the pair turned, cutting through Brewer Street and working in a northerly direction. The streets were comparatively empty—Soho, like its much richer neighbour, Mayfair, not being given to early rising. An odd milk-cart or two were about, pushed by men who seemed about as half-awake as the district they were serving, and paper boys were here and there to be seen scurrying along, only stopping to push the morning sheets under doors, or through letter boxes. Suddenly, that strange sixth sense which seems to be the heritage of both criminals and the men who hunt them, alike, warned him that he was under observation. From some point or other he was being watched by some unseen person! Or was it Regan? That, too, was possible—in the circumstances. Although particularly careful to show no sign that he realized the fact, his eyes sought everywhere in the narrow street to pick up the person who was interested in one or the other of them, but for the life of him he could not. He was quite certain that they were being watched, but whoever was at this shadowing business was certainly an adept.

At the corner of Lexicon Street, at which point he turned to cut through into Dean Street, he gave another seemingly casual, but in reality exceedingly keen glance about him, but could still see no one. Nevertheless, the feeling was stronger than ever upon him that they were under surveillance.

It was as they turned into Dean Street, itself, and crossed the road towards his lodging, that, without the slightest warning, a car shot out of nowhere, for all he could tell, and travelling at an entirely illegal pace, made straight at them. But for a lightning-like grab at Regan, which sent that already shaken person sprawling upon the pavement, and an equally sudden lurch to one side upon his part, it would have unquestionably run them down, and, by the size of the car and the speed it was travelling, with quite fatal results. As it was, its near-side mudguard caught him a glancing blow with such force as to send him in an entirely inelegant, and certainly undignified, dive upon the top of Regan. Before he could get to his feet again, it had accelerated to a still higher speed, shot around Carlisle Street into Soho Square and was gone. Its rear number-plate, he noticed, was so thickly plastered with mud as to be quite undecipherable. Which, as there had been no rain in the last forty-eight hours, told its own story.

He was helping Regan to his feet when, for the first time, he noticed that the occurrence had been watched by a trio of L.C.C. workers engaged in hosing down the gutters from a hydrant a little higher up the street. He was known to them, as he was to most of the denizens of this cosmopolitan quarter.

"Lor' lumme, Inspector," the hose operator exclaimed, "them there bleeders didn't 'arf mean puttin' paid to you! They came straight at you from about fifty yards back."

"It certainly looks as though they were displeased with me for something or other," the inspector said, with his infectious smile. "Though perhaps it may have been a quite unintentional skid," he suggested.

"There was no skid about that," the hose-man informed him, very positively. "They came straight at y', like I'm tellin' you. It might have been a skid if we'd had the hose down that far, but the road's as dry as a flint down there."

"You didn't happen to spot the number on the front plate, I suppose?" McCarthy asked.

Hose-man shook his head. "It was all plastered up," he answered. "If I'd only 'ad me nut screwed on right I'd have hosed it clean, though it wouldn't have been much good at the rate they was going."

"Didn't happen to spot the driver as anyone you knew, I suppose?" McCarthy asked.

The other shook his head.

"No, Inspector," he said. "To tell y' the truth it 'appened so sudden, I was took all of an 'eap."

"There was three of them in the car," one of his mates averred. "One of 'em was that dirty crook, Mascagni. He was crouching back in a corner trying' to 'ide 'isself, but I spotted him."

"You're quite sure of that?" McCarthy asked quietly.

"Certain, Inspector. I'd take me oath on that."

"Well, well," McCarthy said softly. "Our esteemed friend Floriello Mascagni doesn't like us any more, Danny. We've done something to upset him, it seems."

"'E never did 'ave no time for me," the pickpocket growled. "I ain't flash enough for him."

"Perhaps he'll find some for me," McCarthy said grimly. "Or, rather, I'll find some for *him*, before he's so much older," he corrected himself. "And, somehow, I don't think Floriello will like that." He slipped his arm through that of the considerably shaken Regan. "Come on, Daniel, we won't allow this little episode to put us off our appetite, and I've got to be in Soho Square before eight."

But it seemed that there was yet another minute or two to be filched from the rapidly shortening time at the inspector's disposal. He was almost at his own door when a police ambulance, which had been flying down Dean Street towards Shaftesbury Avenue, pulled up beside him with a jerk. In the front of it, beside the driver, was the sergeant who had gone through the house in Soho Square with him, a few hours before.

"Do you know the latest, Inspector?" he hailed in a state of great excitement.

"The latest?" McCarthy questioned back. "The latest of what?"

"Old Joe Anselmi has been found stiff in death in his own back yard, not three-quarters of an hour ago. Some of the neighbours saw the body lying there from their upper windows and notified us. The doctor who ran the rule over him says that he was killed somewhere between midnight and one o'clock this morning as far as he can tell. We know it must have been after half-past eleven, because he was seen going to his yard at that time."

"Joe Anselmi," McCarthy repeated, as staggered a man as he had been in many a long day. "Then—then it couldn't have been he that pushed that coffee-stall out of Soho Square last night, just at the time that that scream was heard."

"That's a certainty," the sergeant snapped, then went on irately: "If the blasted fools had only notified me that he had done so I'd have known something was wrong, because Anselmi had his permit for the coffee-stall to stand where it did, revoked five days ago, owing to the black-out. It hasn't stood there this week."

"So that's how the body was got out of Soho Square last night," McCarthy said thoughtfully.

"Must have been," the sergeant agreed; "there was no other way it could have been managed. And now," he continued, a certain sly look in his eyes, "all y' have to do now, Inspector, is find the body."

"That's been done," McCarthy told him. "I've just come away from the mortuary. Oh, and by the way, Sergeant, for your later guidance I'll just tell you that that scream came from a man, and not a woman. Tell me," he continued quickly, before the sergeant had time to do more than open his mouth in astonishment, "how was poor old Joe killed?"

"Stabbed," the sergeant answered tersely. "And they did it as though they liked doing it, the murdering swine," the sergeant growled. "They made a terrible mess of him. If ever I want to see a man swing—or maybe it's *men*—it's whoever killed Joe Anselmi. He was a decent man."

"He was all that," McCarthy said quietly. "And you'll get your wish, Sergeant. Stand on me, you'll get it before you're so much older. Many's the feed old Joe has stood me when I was a kid about these streets; I reckon hanging his murderers is up to me."

It was not until McCarthy had finished his hastily eaten breakfast—a meal for which the sergeant's news had taken all his appetite—that he turned to the well-nigh ravenous Mr. Regan, who was getting on with it as might a man who never expected to see food again.

"Now, Danny," he said, "as I've told you before, time is precious with me this morning, so begin talking. Out with it—from the moment I left you in Oxford Street until they knocked you cold in Park Lane. Give me the lot, with all the detail you can remember."

◇◇◇

When Inspector McCarthy left "Danny the Dip," that worthy proceeded to put his whole heart and soul into the business before him. To start with, he had unquestionably been upon criminal-pursuit bent when Inspector McCarthy had landed upon him like a bolt from the blue, and he was well aware that the inspector knew just what he was at, as well as he, himself, did. As far as his own mean little mind would permit him, he was not ungrateful for the let-off.

Had "Danny the Dip" been called "Danny the Rat" it would have been no misnomer, for no old buck-rat in his sewer was more cunning than this particular member of the submerged tenth. What his eyes could not tell him, his ears could, and it would indeed have been a clever person who could have deceived either organ.

Along Oxford Street his quarry proceeded, moving, to judge by the sound he made, at the same leisurely pace, and, doubly secure in the total darkness of the black-out, "Danny the Dip" followed. He knew his Oxford Street as well as he did any other main thoroughfare of the metropolis; to him in light or fog of the worst possible pea-soup variety, they were all as open a book as the stairs to his third-floor back-bedroom. At the corner of Marylebone Lane, leading through to Wigmore Street, the man stopped and appeared to be waiting until a constable whose solid tread told his trade unmistakably came up with him. For a moment or two they stood conferring; the man evidently making some enquiry.

For a moment or two the unpleasant thought crossed the pickpocket's mind that the man had discovered that he was being followed and was making some complaint about it—the inspector had said that he was a fly bird, and one who couldn't be taken liberties with. Mr. Regan did not like this conference a little bit; even the safeguard that he was on a job for Detective Inspector McCarthy did not remove a momentary qualm.

But after a moment or two his quick ears told him that the two had moved apart; the policeman proceeding at the regulation pace upon his beat, while the other slightly quickened his steps in the direction of a telephone-booth which Dan knew stood at a little distance along Marylebone Lane. Into this the man went and, assisted by the beam of a torch he carried, dialled a number and remained there a full three minutes.

Leaving the box, he returned to Oxford Street and, at an even slower pace than before, proceeded to cross the road and move in the direction of the Marble Arch. Promptly his shadow followed on, making no more sound than a cat stalking a bird. At the corner of Park Lane the man made a sudden stop. After a moment or two, he lit a cigarette; the light of his match giving Danny a chance to make sure he was on his right mark; then he crossed slowly over to the park corner of the lane and there stood waiting—the glow of his cigarette was as good as a friendly lamp-post to his shadower.

Some five minutes passed without his quarry moving, which halt was as blood and tears to "Danny the Dip," for across at the corner of the Edgware Road, his almost cat-like eyes showed him a faint haze of light which told him that the coffee-stall which usually stood there was still in full swing. The very thought of it augmented the pangs of hunger which, rat-like, were gnawing at him to a terrible extent. So much did his discomfiture increase that, seeing no sign of movement on the part of his quarry, he determined to take a chance. He had no fear of being knocked down by any traffic at this time of the morning, and in the circumstances, so, keeping his eye upon the glowing end of that cigarette, he made a quick dash to the stall, spent two of his shillings in sandwiches, and was about to take a chance upon a hastily gulped cup of coffee when the light disappeared.

Grabbing up his bag of sandwiches and his change he rushed across the road to the point at which he had last seen the light; there was nothing of strategy about his movements, all he wanted to do was pick his man up again. Hurrying around the corner and wolfing at his food as he went, he almost ran smack into the object of Inspector McCarthy's interest. He had simply drawn back into the shadow of one of the park trees, and at the moment that Danny came up with him, lighted another cigarette.

He took not the slightest notice of the figure which hurried past him. Going on a bit, and in something of a quandary, Danny crossed the road as far as the corner of North Row, from which point he kept his eye fixed upon the glow of the cigarette end, and wished the man would make up his mind to move in some direction or other.

Presently the light commenced to move along Park Lane, in the direction of Piccadilly; the smoker appearing to travel in the same calm, leisurely manner that he had before. Inwardly, Danny blessed that glowing cigarette tip;

it was as good as a lighthouse to him. Letting him get a little distance ahead of him, he, too, crossed the road, and in the same soundless way followed up behind.

Follower and followed were about half way down Park Lane when a big car which showed practically no lights at all came swiftly up behind him, then pulled up with a scream of maltreated brakes. Before he could realize what was happening, three men jumped out of it and made a rush at him. The very swiftness of their attack was sufficient to tell him that they meant business and without hesitation he let fly a quick punch at the first to reach him. The blow was picked off with ease, and in the next instant a cast-iron fist descended upon the back of his neck, sending him reeling, half-dazed, back to the fence. In the next moment something, an iron bar he believed, came down upon his skull, and millions of lights danced before his eyes, then it seemed to him that he went sliding down a long, long tube of what seemed to be black velvet—into nothingness.

That was all he knew until he found himself being led by a "flattie" into a police station somewhere or other, and heard the man tell his inspector that he had picked him up wandering about on Hampstead Heath. In a dazed sort of way he gathered that the body of someone who had been murdered had been found close by him, and the idea seemed to be that he had had something to do with the crime. As well as he could, he endeavoured to explain that he had been doing a job for Detective Inspector McCarthy of Scotland Yard, and if somebody would ring up the telephone number he gave they would find that everything was O.K. as far as he was concerned. After that, he must have gone off into a faint or something, because he remembered nothing else until they were trying to pull him together to be brought back to the West End.

◇◇◇

Such was the story that "Danny the Dip" had to tell to his patron, and that every word of it was truth and nothing but the truth, that experienced officer needed no telling. The evidence to that effect was seated in front of him.

Chapter X

McCarthy is Taken Off the Case!

Inspector McCarthy arrived again at the house in Soho Square a good half-hour before anyone else—with the exception of the men on duty, back and front, there. He found that the uniformed constables had been relieved by plain-clothes men from Vine Street, who had taken up certain positions in the square from which they could watch the front of the house without seeming to be in any way connected with it. The door itself had been carefully cleansed down by his own instructions after the fingerprint men had done with it, so that, save for the deep red stains of the blood which had sunk into the stone steps and the area, there was no exterior sign of the ghastly crime connected with it.

Making his way first to the rear, he went carefully over the ground in the hope of finding foot-spoor, but out of it all he could find only one thing which seemed to have any value, and that was that the man who had passed through the house—presumably the dual murderer—had worn shoes with an extremely light sole. He would have said dress shoes. The hall itself gave no results whatever when subjected to an intensified search. It was covered with linoleum which, had it been daily polished, might have shown a more detailed impression, but it obviously was washed down daily, and therefore had no impressionable surface.

His first job had been to draw the front door bolts, obviously shot by the murderer when he had made his entry into the house. Until that was done no one could gain entry.

The "dabs" men had reported that as far as the hall, banisters of the staircases, front and back doors were concerned, they could find no trace of prints likely to be of any use whatever in the case.

He was just finishing his examination when the first post delivery shot a mass of correspondence through into the wire basket fixed behind the letter slot in the front door. Taking it out, he carefully examined the names of the parties to whom they were addressed and checked them up with the board containing a list of office-renters which was affixed to the wall of the hall.

These were, for the greater part, agents in a small way for various forms of industrial requirements, a small typewriting and duplicating agency, and one firm to whose activities there was no clue at all. This was a certain Madame Rohner, a name which savoured strongly of German origin, though the "Madame" seemed to suggest a French connection. But the only one piece of correspondence there was for the lady—in an open envelope and bearing a halfpenny stamp—turned out to be from some firm of whom McCarthy had never heard, simply stating that the goods as ordered had already been despatched and should be delivered by the time she received this epistle. As to what those goods might be there was no indication whatever.

McCarthy's examination of this particular correspondence was broken in upon by the sound of a key in the front door Yale lock. In the next moment it was opened and a youth entered who, doubtless, was the one spoken of by the sergeant. His amazement at finding the inspector seated upon the lower step of the staircase, and by him the morning correspondence, was profound; it was in no degree lessened when he heard of the crime which had been perpetrated there since his leaving it the evening before.

But although the inspector questioned him steadily for a good half-hour, nothing in the slightest degree suspicious could be got from him concerning any of the individuals, or firms, renting the offices. They sounded to be very plain, straightforward business people, and not in the least likely to be in any way connected with the crime in any shape or form.

Going to the back door McCarthy called in the C.I.D. man who had been stationed at the back gate.

"Check up on everyone as they come in," he ordered. "Go into the nature of their business and, in particular, who it's done with, and if they have any definitely foreign connections." He turned again to the still staring youth.

"Have you a master-key to these offices?" he asked, to be informed that he had not. Each of the renters had his, or her, own key, which was given to them when they completed satisfactory arrangements for tenantry. If there was such a thing as a master-key he did not know of it. If it existed it would be in the hands of Mr. Morris Bavinsky, the owner of the place. That gentleman only put in appearance once weekly—on Saturday morning to collect his rents.

"Now, this lady, Madame Rohner?" McCarthy inquired. "What was her particular line of business?"

That also the youth, by name, Hubert Wilkins, could not tell him. Whatever it was, it took her away from her office a great deal, for at times days elapsed without her putting in an appearance there.

"Did she have a good amount of correspondence?" McCarthy asked.

He was told that the lady's correspondence was not heavy, and mostly seemed to come from the Continent. She had letters from France, Germany, Italy, and other still more remote countries. Upon this point Wilkins was very positive as, being an enthusiastic philatelist, he invariably cadged the stamps from the envelopes.

"Now, just let me understand this," McCarthy pursued. "Each person renting offices here in this building is provided with a key to the front door?"

"Yes, sir; in case they want to come back and work in their offices after closing hours."

"Therefore anyone holding such a key can come in at any hour of the day or night that pleases them?"

"Yes, sir."

"Are there any other keys extant that you know of; keys not been returned by former tenants, for example? People giving up their offices in recent months who've forgotten, or neglected, to hand them in?"

There were not. That, it seemed, was a thing about which Mr. Bavinsky was very particular. He, Wilkins, had to collect them before the tenant departed.

"Check up on all these keys, as well," he instructed the C.I.D. man.

In response to a question as to what manner of woman Madame Rohner was, he was informed that she was a very handsome lady, always particularly well dressed and seemed to be in no way short of money. For any little service done her she invariably tipped handsomely; in fact, in Wilkins' opinion, it was a pleasure to see her come into the place.

McCarthy's next question concerned the two ladies who, he understood, did the charing after the offices were closed. Had they keys?

They had not, it seemed. They arrived before the front door was shut for the night at six o'clock, did their work and left by the back door which, having a spring lock, they pulled to after them. They merely cleaned the hall and stairways and had nothing to do with the charing of the interior of the offices unless especially engaged to do so by the tenants themselves. In most cases, it was invariably done during the lunch hour or some other time of the day most convenient to the occupiers.

"Then if, for argument, Madame Rohner went away, or at any rate was absent for a few days, as you say she is in the habit of being, wouldn't it be possible for you or anyone else to get into her office without forcing an entrance?"

"No, sir."

"In which case," McCarthy said, "we'll just go upstairs to her offices and see if *we* can't get in without forcing an entry. You shall come in with me, just to see I don't pinch anything."

Outside the door, upon which was a small plate which merely gave the name of the tenant and no indication of her business, he took a pick-lock from his pocket. In less time than it takes to tell, and certainly less than permitted Mr. Wilkins to see how it was done, McCarthy shot the tumbler, turned the handle and walked in. The first thing to strike him was that scent which had hung about the outer doorway hours before!

"Why, it's—everything's gone!" Wilkins exclaimed in astonishment.

"And just what d'ye mean by that?" McCarthy questioned.

"Why, when I brought letters up after the five o'clock delivery yesterday afternoon there were papers all over the table—letters, and things like that. They're all gone!"

McCarthy pointed to the grate in which there was nothing but a pile of black paper ash.

"Yes," he said wearily, "they're all gone, right enough! Too far gone for us to ever be able to make anything out of them."

A search of the cupboards in the room, and the drawers in the office table at which the "lady" had worked, revealed the fact that they were bare. Madame had evidently made a very thorough clearance of everything in that office, save the actual furniture and the typewriter, between five o'clock in the evening and the present moment. Between that time and one o'clock in the morning, McCarthy would have said—unless, of course, someone had done it for her.

Kneeling before the grate, he stirred the ashes gently with his finger in the hope of finding even the most minute solid fragment which might provide a lead as to Madame Rohner's business, or other connections. But the job had been done with such thoroughness that his search proved entirely futile.

"Then there's only one thing for it, Wilkins," he said. "We've got to find this Madame Rohner, and you seem to be the only one who can assist us to do it. I suppose you're a pretty tough sort of person—go to the pictures and see all sorts of gruesome and hard-boiled things?"

"Who—me, sir?" Mr. Wilkins drew up his thin frame until it looked two inches taller than it was. "Yes, I don't mind anything. I've seen Frankenstein and Dracula and…"

"That's tough enough for anything," McCarthy remarked and led him downstairs, first relocking the door with his pick-lock. Beckoning another of the plain-clothes men at the front of the place he gave him quiet instructions. "Grab the first taxi you can and take him along to the mortuary," he said, *sotto voce*, "and see if he can identify a corpse found on Hampstead Heath last night as Madame Rohner." From his pocket he took the small parcel which contained the wig. "See that that's put on before he views the body," he instructed. "Phone me the moment he identifies, and bring me the wig back here as soon as possible."

Exactly seven minutes later a call came through for him

from the mortuary. Wilkins had identified the body as that of the mysterious tenant, Madame Rohner.

"How did he take it?" McCarthy asked.

"Just managed to get it out," the C.I.D. man told him, "then fainted dead away. They're bringing him round with a drop of brandy."

McCarthy grinned quietly. "Wonderful how tough they are—when the gore is on the screen. Hurry up with that wig."

At ten minutes past nine, Inspector McCarthy found out by a search of the books of the wigmakers in question, that the late lamented Heinrich had made the wig some four years before, for one Oscar Schmidt, an actor who had come over from Berlin to play in a season of short German plays at the Little Theatre. The actor in question had not returned to Germany with the other members of the company, having contracted pneumonia. He died after a very short illness and was buried at Kensal Green within three weeks of his arrival here. What had become of the wig after his decease was more than anyone could say.

"And that's that!" McCarthy murmured as he left the shop. "We're up against a brick wall as far as that particular angle goes."

A call to the Bloomsbury residence of Sir William Haynes, brought that most efficient person to the phone in what was unmistakably a state of considerable agitation.

"Meet me at the Yard in half an hour, Mac!" he ordered peremptorily, and before McCarthy could get in a word.

"With all the will in the world, it can't be done!" McCarthy told him bluntly. "As you know I've been on this Soho murder job since one o'clock this morning, and I'm just waiting for…"

"It doesn't matter what you're waiting for," the A.C. snapped in a most unusually arbitrary manner. "The superintendent can handle that."

"But he's out of town this morning," McCarthy informed him, "and this case is developing big…"

"He'll be recalled," the A.C. cut in sharply. "You be in my office in half an hour. Take that as positive orders. I don't care how the Soho case is developing. The job waiting for you is bigger. You be there."

With a quite unstifled expletive, McCarthy hung up, then hailed the first taxi he could find and was driven to the Yard.

Chapter XI

Motive

In that pleasant room overlooking the Embankment in which the Assistant Commissioner performed his duties, that hard-worked official was pacing up and down in a manner which suggested to McCarthy the peregrinations of a tiger, newly caged.

"'Tis a dam' queer thing, Bill," McCarthy was saying with as much bad temper as ever his friend had known him to show, "how the divil this sort of thing happens. Damme, don't tell me that the highly-placed officer to whom these things were entrusted just left them out at the pavement-edge in his open car while he nipped into his club to have a drink! That's the sort of thing ye read of in the papers every day. The last I seem to remember had something to do with a Naval Code Book."

"This wasn't half as stupid as anything of that sort, Mac," Sir William told him hurriedly. "These Anti-Aircraft Defence Plans—and don't forget they embraced the whole system for Great Britain and are invaluable to the enemy—were stolen from Whitehall and unfortunately there's no doubt but that they were stolen direct. The plans had been accurately checked over by General Sir Marcus Pettingill, who was in charge of the whole business, and had been put, and carefully locked into, the safe in his room in Whitehall from which he went no farther than across a corridor to a conference. He was away less than half an hour and remained in his room for the rest of the afternoon. At about half-past five he had occasion to refer to them again, reopened the safe, which certainly had not been touched by any one official and they were gone.

"From that moment to this not the slightest trace of them have they been able to find. Every soul in the place who could possibly have been anywhere near that part of the building has been questioned, but without results. It means that unless we can prevent them being got out of Britain every disposition must be altered for others, obviously not so good or they would have been chosen first, and many months of preparatory work rendered absolutely useless."

"Yes, that's fairly obvious," McCarthy said thoughtfully. "Dammit, Bill, that's good espionage work on their part, isn't it?"

Through the inspector's mind a certain query was beginning to percolate; could there possibly be any connection between the murder of this mysterious "Madame Rohner" and these stolen plans? That the disguised man was here for espionage he was quite satisfied in his own mind. However, for the moment he kept his thoughts to himself. Time enough to air his suspicions when he knew more of what had happened in Whitehall.

"Was the door of the general's office left open while he went to this conference?" he asked.

Haynes shook his head negatively. "It has a snap-lock which, of course, becomes effective the moment the door is closed," he informed McCarthy. "It has to be opened again by a key by the general himself. He has the only one—with the exception of the master-key in the hands of an absolutely reliable official who is always upon the scene when the room is open during the whole time the office is being cleaned."

"What's the safe like?" McCarthy asked.

"You shall see it for yourself," Haynes told him. "I can tell you that it is one of Chubb's latest combination patents. That one there"—he pointed to an extremely solid safe which stood in one corner of his room—"is a mere paraffin can in comparison with it."

McCarthy sat up alertly.

"That proves class work, Bill," he said seriously. "To get into the place at all, gain entry to that room, open the safe, remove those plans and then get out again in less than half an hour is to say two things. The first, that the man must have had some dashed fine first-hand information as to just where what he wanted was to be found, for one thing. For a second, he must have been one of their really crack men to handle that safe in the way that he did; no little tinpot spy is going to tackle a job of that kind."

"That is only too obvious," Haynes said ruefully. "Hence the necessity for speedy action. If the spy in question was clever enough to get them in the time that he did, it won't overtax his resources to find some way to have them out of the country."

"True enough," McCarthy agreed. "I needn't ask whether the S.B. men have been up on their toes on the job."

"On their toes!" Haynes echoed. "My dear fellow, I've not so long since left their superintendent, and every available man has been at it from within a quarter of an hour of the discovery of the theft. Every German man or woman not already interned and in any way under the slightest suspicion, has been rounded up, but so far, all of them have cast-iron alibis. No, there's been no time wasted, I can assure you of that. And I may tell you," he added in a different tone, "that it's a very big feather in your cap that, even in a moment of desperation, the Special Branch chiefs should have applied to the H.Q. for your services."

"It's very nice of them," McCarthy said with a wry smile, "but I'd rather be——However, never mind about that. I suppose the room in question is just as it is when the loss was discovered—hasn't been cleaned out, or any damn silly routine foolishness of that kind?"

"Good heavens, no, man! The place, after it was gone over for fingerprints, was at once almost hermetically sealed: a guard placed over doors, and even outside windows. You'll find it exactly as it was."

"Thank heaven for that!" McCarthy said fervently, and added whimsically: "The good old game of locking the stable door after the horse is gone. If you're ready we'll get there right away."

As they walked through Cannon Row towards Whitehall, McCarthy gave the A.C. a further quick *résumé* of the happenings in Soho Square after that scream had rung out, and the later and still more extraordinary developments.

"I may be altogether wrong, Bill," he concluded, "but I can't shake off the hunch which struck me the moment I set eyes again in the square on that man we saw at Signora Spadoglia's. I'm certain that in some way or other he's connected with the crimes, if not himself the actual dual murderer. What happened to Regan, and the discovery of the body only confirms it."

"A most extraordinary business," Sir William commented. "But still there's no actual evidence to connect him with the assault on Regan. He certainly wasn't in the car."

"No, but it's my belief that he phoned for it from Marylebone Lane. And I've another hunch, Bill," McCarthy said sombrely, "and that is that… but I'll let that go for awhile. At any rate until I've taken a look over this room."

Not another word passed his lips until they entered the portals of the ravaged building and were led by a high official to the door of that room which had been so mysteriously burgled the afternoon before. The man on duty before the door stepped to one side and the official in question was about to turn the key in the lock when McCarthy stopped him.

"If you don't mind," he said quietly, "I'd like to be the first to enter this room. Sometimes just a sight of things as they've been left tells you something."

Throwing open the door he stepped into the room. As he did so a waft of heavy air from the sealed interior passed across his face. A strange, most satisfied look came into his eyes, and he uttered a soft "Ah!" which made the Assistant Commissioner step towards him quickly.

"What is it, Mac?" he asked sharply. "Seen something that gives you a lead?"

"No," McCarthy said quietly, "not seen—smelt. For some little time now I've had the idea that I knew who did this job—now I'm sure of it. And I know now the motive behind the murder," he went on slowly; "I know now *why* he was killed."

"He? Who? You're talking in parables, Mac," the A.C. protested irritably.

"To you—maybe," McCarthy returned. "To myself—no. 'Madame Rohner' worked this job—that is why 'she' was murdered."

For the thing that had halted him as he entered that room, stopped him dead in his tracks as might a bullet, was the pleasant odour of that same scent which had invaded his nostrils on the doorstep of the house in Soho Square, and again at the mortuary. It had been rendered doubly pungent by the fact that the room, both windows and doors, had been tightly closed ever since the pseudo woman who had robbed it had been in the place. It had been equally strong in that upper office in Soho.

"Come on," he said, "I'm done here for the time being. My work lies elsewhere."

Only one thing the inspector asked to be shown before leaving the building, and that was a facsimile of the sheets which had been stolen.

"The material on which the dispositions were drawn or printed on, I mean," he explained.

He was shown a sheet of a sort of extremely fine oiled paper of a deep blue colour. It was about two feet square in size, and six of them, the number stolen, folded tightly together could have been concealed upon anyone without the slightest risk of detection. McCarthy studied them for a moment in silence, then, wetting the tips of the thumb and finger of his right hand, rubbed the surface softly; after a moment or two a blue tinge showed up the ball of his thumb.

"That's all," he said abruptly and was off out into Whitehall again. Sir William pounded after him, wondering inwardly what crazy idea was going to seize upon McCarthy next.

At the pavement edge McCarthy hailed the first taxi he saw running towards Piccadilly, which vehicle pulled up promptly. It happened to be driven by that particular protégée of McCarthy's, taxi owner-driver "Big Bill" Withers, who saluted both gentlemen with the deepest respect. But for once the ever-genial McCarthy merely grunted a response, got in, gave his orders to be driven to the mortuary, then passed into silence, staring frowningly at the floor of the taxi. Haynes also kept silence—when McCarthy was in that mood he was thinking at high pressure and the less interruption he got the better.

Arrived at the grim building, McCarthy made for the mortuary-keeper's office and demanded at once the now cellophane-covered and carefully docketed packet of clothes which had been taken from the body of the murdered "Madame Rohner." No sooner had he unfastened the package than again a waft of that perfume came to him, even over the unpleasant one of dried blood.

"Smell that," he requested Haynes curtly. "Didn't you get exactly that same scent when the door of that room was opened?"

"I did," the A.C. responded instantly. "What does it mean, Mac?"

"It means that the man who was murdered in Soho Square, the one to whom these clothes belong, was the thief. But I'm hoping to find definite traces of something else which will prove it beyond all doubt."

Over every inch of the top portions of the silken underwear he went with the aid of a pocket magnifying-glass, to be rewarded at length by finding upon one of the garments a faint blue stain which corresponded exactly with the one upon his thumb. A moment or two later he had found a tiny fray of the same colour.

"There's the whole story, Bill," he said. "The man having got the prints, folded them and pushed them down the front of his dress. The warmth of his body loosened some of that dye, and left the imprint. The killer must have had a fair idea as to where he would find what he wanted, and in tearing them from where they were hidden separated just this tiny fragment of frayed edge from one of the sheets. To find them we've got to lay hands upon the murderer of this man who masqueraded in London as 'Madame Rohner.'"

"Rohner…Rohner…?" Haynes repeated. "I seem to know that name somewhere quite apart from your mention of it."

But McCarthy was already away upon another angle. Hurrying to the slab upon which the murdered man lay he turned down the cover and examined the finger-tips of both hands. Upon those of the right hand he found definite traces of the same stain.

"That settles the point finally, Bill," he said. "We've got the thief—and much good he is to us."

"What's your next move, now, Mac?" Sir William asked anxiously. "Is there no other clue to give you a lead of some sort or kind?"

"A lace handkerchief without even a monogram on it, and a bloodstained knife without fingerprints or marks of any kind," McCarthy said. "There's nothing whatever in the place in Soho Square but a heap of charred ashes, and even they belonged to the murdered man and certainly won't give me a clue to the one who killed him. I daresay one of these great detectives of fiction would see a dozen leads in what I've got, but dam'd if I can see an inch ahead of me."

"Which means that you've really no idea which way to turn now, Mac?" Haynes questioned, the same anxious note in his voice.

McCarthy paused before answering.

"Well," he said reflectively, "there's a certain gentleman I want a word with who was one of the party who tried to run over me this morning. It might have been Dan Regan they were after, but I have my doubts."

"Ha! That's an idea," the A.C. exclaimed eagerly. "You can demand…"

"Demand, *nothing!*" McCarthy interrupted. "If I as much as let fall a suggestion that I knew him to be one of them, that would be the end of it. I'll have to go to work in a divil of a roundabout way with him."

"Then, for heaven's sake, get a start upon him without loss of time. You've no idea the state of mind the powers that be are in over this business."

McCarthy smiled. "I can imagine," he returned. "I've seen 'jitters' in high places before to-day. The best thing you can do," he continued, "is to get back and cheer them with the news that the great Detective Inspector McCarthy has already discovered the thief and found him as dead as ever he's likely to be. The next thing is to find his killer. After that, there *may*, with a bit of luck, be a chance of recovering the stolen sheets. Off you go, Bill, and lighten their hearts. And don't take Withers; I'll want him."

"Isn't there *anything* you can suggest that I can be doing to help?" Haynes asked almost pleadingly.

McCarthy ran his hand over his glossy black hair a moment while he thought.

"Yes," he said. "Try and have the call traced that was put in at the Marylebone Lane box at almost one-twenty this morning. In the old days it would have been easy, but since the automatic dial it's a well-nigh hopeless job. But have a go at it all the same."

"And if I fail?"

McCarthy shrugged his shoulders.

"Just sit down and twiddle your fingers until you hear from me. It's all you *can* do, Bill, whether you like it or not."

"I can't say that I fancy the prospect," Haynes groaned.

"While you're at it make very sure that all the air and sea ports are closely watched for anything like our icy-eyed friend getting away to one of the neutral countries open to travellers from here. Mail to Germany is out of the question but a tip to the Post Office people to closely watch any Continental stuff won't do any harm."

"Pure routine in the last case, and done long ago," Haynes said. "But I'll put through an urgent order for all officials at the ports to keep a keen look-out for anything answering the description of our blind-looking friend of last night. I think I can remember him well enough to set him out fairly accurately. After that," he added, "I think I'll get out of the way for a while—on the same urgent business, of course.

I don't fancy frantic calls every five minutes or so to know what's fresh in the case."

"I don't blame you," McCarthy said.

"What about Verrey's in Regent Street at about one o'clock for a spot of lunch?" the A.C. put insidiously. "You may have something fresh to report by then."

"As it's just after twelve now," the inspector said, with a glance at his wrist-watch, "I very much doubt it. The well-known Luck of the McCarthys is good, but it's not as good as all *that*. Anyhow," he added whimsically, "I've eaten twice in the twenty-four hours, and that's as much, and more, as any C.I.D. man can expect these strenuous days and black-out nights. However, as I see ye've the urge on y' to buy me a really tip-top lunch I'll not turn the offer down altogether, but if I'm not at Verrey's by half-past one you'll know that I've got my nose to the ground on the job—probably inter-viewing Signor Floriello Mascagni."

"Mascagni!" Haynes exclaimed in considerable surprise. "That's the fellow who came into Signora Spadoglia's last night and dropped you some information, isn't it?"

"The same," McCarthy informed him.

"What's he got to do with it?"

"That's what I want to know," McCarthy answered equably. "On your way, Bill. On your way. You're holding up the processes of the Law!"

Chapter XII

A Chance Encounter

For a solid hour now McCarthy had been cruising the environs of Soho in Withers' taxi-cab, but without picking up the slightest trace of the man he wanted. In and out of wine shops and small Italian restaurants favoured by the tough brotherhood of whom Flo. Mascagni was the undisputed head, he drifted, but never a word of the Soho-Italian could he pick up. Whether Mascagni had deemed it wise to hop out of town, or otherwise lie low after the attempt upon him that morning, McCarthy did not know, but he doubted it, since the gangster had no reason for thinking that he had been spotted by either of the intended victims. Knowing Inspector McCarthy as he did, he would have been quite certain in his own mind that a police "drag" would have been out for him within half an hour of the occurrence, and as nothing of the kind had happened he would see no reason for flight, or even temporarily absenting himself from his usual haunts.

"'Ow'd it be if I was to leave you up the street a bit and take a mike into that dive of Fasoli's, guv'nor?" Withers suggested. "That there bugpit as is called the *Circolo Venezia*. That's the main 'ang-out of Mascagni's mob, though it's kept pretty dark, and they don't go near there much before night."

McCarthy nodded his agreement. "Good idea, Withers," he said. "I hadn't forgotten that hole, but I knew dashed well I, personally, should get no information out of it. But it might be different with you. Hop along and see what you can find out."

In five minutes he was back again. "There's a race meetin' at Cheltenham to-day, guv'nor," he reported, "and 'im an' 'is gang is away at it. At any rate, the mob's gorn, and Fasoli thinks 'e's wiv 'em, which is most likely."

"More than likely, Withers," McCarthy agreed. "They wouldn't have to take a train up there before ten in the morning. That would have left plenty of time for Mascagni to have caught it after—after I saw him early this morning. In which case," he continued, "luncheon at Verrey's seems to be indicated. While I'm at it you'd better park your car around in Marlborough Street and get something to eat yourself. Don't get too near to the police court, though, or they may have you inside."

"Don't worry, guv'nor, I've been there twice and that was any amount and too damn much," Mr. Withers rejoined, grinning hugely. "An' as far as lunch goes, mine's allus ready at any hour durin' openin' times. A couple o' good pulls on the beer pump, an' it's all cooked and served."

"Don't overdo it, Withers," McCarthy warned. "The ways of motor transgressors are not easy these times."

"You're tellin' *me*, guv'nor!" Mr. Withers exclaimed. "Not 'arf they ain't! Fair persecutin', I call 'em."

Arrived in Regent Street McCarthy proceeded to that famous restaurant, sacred to the rich and fashionable, and found Haynes already installed at a table and waiting for him. Quite a number of Continentals of note were, he saw, taking their accustomed late *déjeuner*. It was a favourite house for that.

Among them, seated alone at a table in one of the windows, was one of the most beautiful women McCarthy remembered to have seen in many a long day. She was simply, but most expensively gowned and, taken all in all, was indeed a pleasurable sight for any eye. As he took his seat she turned and, apparently noticing Haynes for the first time, bowed to him. He promptly responded with an obeisance of the deepest respect. For a moment McCarthy thought that Haynes was going to cross to the window and have a word with her, but he gave his attention to the waiter who came forward with a menu card.

"Who is that lady?" he asked, when the ordering of the lunch was completed.

"The Baroness Lena Eberhardt," Haynes told him in a confidential whisper. "Quite an old friend of mine—by which I mean I've met her dozens of times at different social functions."

"German?" McCarthy asked casually. She looked it to him, very definitely.

"Good heavens, no—Austrian. Hates the Nazi gang like poison. Viennese—one of the real old Austrian nobility. She's lived here for some years now—two or three at least. Has a fine old house in Grosvenor Square."

"Has she, begad," McCarthy said. "Then she's a dashed sight luckier than most of the old Austrian nobility. They haven't any houses anywhere at the moment—or money, either."

"She was lucky enough to get all hers out long before Hitler ever thought of the *anschluss*," Haynes said. "And it was no little, I can assure you. The baroness is a really wealthy woman."

"I could find it in my heart to wish I was something similar," McCarthy said, helping himself to sole. "I notice," he said quietly, "that the lady is still eyeing you covertly, Bill. Almost as if she thinks you ought to go over and have a word with her."

"Which p'raps I should," the A.C. said. "I've been her guest a good many times. Excuse me for a moment."

He crossed to the table and, for some three or four minutes spoke to the lady, who, while conversing with him animatedly, somehow seemed to have her very beautiful eyes fixed upon McCarthy. This was so to such an extent that it made that extremely good-looking gentleman somewhat self-conscious. Presently Haynes returned.

"Mac," he said, "I'm requested to bring you over for introduction. The baroness has heard of you and read in the Press of some of your exploits, and she's most anxious to meet you."

"Meet me!" McCarthy gasped. "My hat, Bill, I'm too shy to talk to anyone, let alone a society woman who I'd have to mind my P's and Q's in front of. And too hungry as well."

"After you've finished lunch, of course. The baroness is in no hurry—she's really killing time till she meets a friend. Come on," he urged. "You can't get out of it and you need only stay a few minutes. Just do the pleasant for a minute or two—she's really a most charming woman."

The meal over and the bill settled, Haynes got up and moved to the lady's table. Reluctantly McCarthy followed and, while inwardly wishing her at the other end of the earth at the moment, permitted no sign of his true feelings to show upon his countenance. In a moment or two he was chatting as gaily with her as though he had known her all his life.

"You will never guess what I have been doing this morning," she remarked with an extraordinarily soft, musical laugh which McCarthy found extremely fascinating. "It is perhaps unwise that I should tell it to you two gentlemen of the police, since I understand that according to your foolish, so funny laws, it is quite illegal. I am therefore a criminal."

"A very beautiful one!" McCarthy murmured gallantly. "What is the crime, Baroness?"

"I have been having my fortune told," she answered. "Once every month, if not more often, I go to my favourite soothsayer to read me the crystal, and that, I understand, is a crime in this country. Is it not so?"

"Pure charlatanism," Haynes laughed, but she shook her head in a very decided negative. The Baroness Eberhardt could be unshakably determined if she chose, McCarthy thought.

"Not my woman," she said. "I knew her in Vienna before she came here. My Madame Rohner, as she calls herself in London, is no charlatan—far from it."

At the mention of that name the inspector felt himself go rigid, yet not by the quiver of a muscle did he permit the smile upon his face to alter. It seemed to him, though he would have freely admitted that it might be pure imagination on his part, that the baroness had been watching him covertly as she had uttered the name; at any rate she had turned fully in his direction. It struck him as an extraordinary coincidence that that name, which he, personally, with all his knowledge of London and its West End, had never encountered before, should come so fluently from this lady's lips at just this particular moment.

Haynes, smiling almost fatuously at the lady, appeared to have noticed nothing; the name was not engraved upon his mind as it was upon McCarthy's. Some instinctive warning shot through the inspector's brain as he listened, to make no mention of the fact that it had any significance for him whatever; to just keep on smirking like a grinning idiot and see in what way this strange situation would develop.

But one thing came back instantly to his memory. In the house at Soho Square he had searched the telephone book to find only one subscriber of that name in it—the man masquerading as a woman who had been so brutally murdered the night before. He determined to lay a little trap.

"'Tis a marvel to me how these people keep going, Baroness, when you think of all the little pitfalls the Metropolitan Police, and the Yard, for that matter, set for them. I suppose you have to make your appointments in advance by telephone, and they get you to nip in and out again as quickly and covertly as maybe."

"Oh, yes, I always call her up by phone, of course; one has to give her plenty of notice one's coming. She has a large clientele of us believers in the occult—despite your foolish official opinions."

"I can see that we shall have to tighten up our Post Office connections in that respect," Haynes said smilingly. "Can't allow our friends to put themselves in the position of being pounced upon while they're having their futures unfolded to them. The omens were happy in your case, I hope?"

The baroness smiled. "Oh, quite," she answered. "At least," she amended, "as good as I can reasonably expect them to be in these dreadful times. Yes, this morning's revelations were quite pro—how do you say the word?—propitious."

"A lie!" were the two words that snapped through McCarthy's brain with the sharpness of a physical blow, though the engaging smile never for an instant left his lips. Since he knew positively that there was but one Madame Rohner listed in the telephone book, it was a manifest impossibility for this woman to have communicated with her by telephone that morning, and still less to have visited her. Somewhere behind this mention of the pseudo woman there was a definite meaning, one not in any way clear to him. Haynes, as far as he knew and that was almost certainty, had not mentioned the Soho Square murder; he had not had the time to have done so, for one thing, and, as far as that went, no man in the world more secretive concerning Departmental business than its second in command. More than ever would that be so since the case had linked up with the Whitehall business.

That this woman, Austrian baroness, or whatever she might be, knew *something* of that crime, was the thought that was beginning to creep into his mind. In some way or other she must also have learned that he was handling it, otherwise the mention of the name had no significance at all. Either she had brought that in as a deliberate feeler to find out something, and that something whether he had so far been able to get at the real identity of the "woman" who had been murdered, or it was meaningless. The possibility was that she had expected him to seize avidly upon the mention of the name and commence bombarding her with questions, out of which she would have extracted information she would not dare to ask openly. It was a point on which he must make himself exceedingly sure before going much further.

He was about to get up and excuse himself upon the grounds of work to be done, when, glancing through the wire blinds which gave privacy to the café, and with which all windows opening on to the street were fitted, he saw something which stopped him most effectually. Crossing Regent Street towards the place, and at an angle which suggested that he was coming from the direction of Oxford Street, was the man he had been seeking—Floriello Mascagni. Reaching the pavement, he took a glance at his wrist watch, then moved directly for the corner of the window behind which the table occupied by the baroness was set. He passed as close to it as it was possible, and, as he did so, McCarthy both saw and heard him give a distinct knock upon the glass pane.

That knock was not only distinct, but peculiarly *distinctive*; a quick double, then two single taps. To the inspector, watching Mascagni who he knew could not possibly see him, or any one else at that table through the wire blind, it was as intriguing a business as anything else which had to do with this extraordinary case.

That it was a signal of some sort or other he was as positive as he could well be, but who to? Certainly not himself, or Haynes, who could not be seen, and it seemed ridiculous to suppose that it could be to the wealthy Austrian aristocrat, the Baroness Eberhardt. As it happened, she had been right in his line of sight the moment Mascagni had knocked; as a matter of fact she had been the nearest to the Soho-Italian at that moment; indeed, nothing but the thick pane of glass had actually separated the two. Entirely without intent McCarthy's eyes had been as much upon her as they had been upon Mascagni. But not a muscle of her beautiful face had moved at the sound. Indeed, she appeared to have been perfectly unconscious of it. It was a queer business altogether, for that it had been no idle drumming of the fingers against the windows in passing he was quite certain. The whole thing had McCarthy guessing—and thinking.

Another thing also McCarthy saw through the wire blinds, and that was the appearance of Mr. William Withers, minus his vehicle, at the corner of the street almost opposite. He saw the huge taxi-man light a cigarette, and look about him in a manner which suggested filling up time until his patron was ready to appear, then suddenly the Withers' orbs fixed upon something upon the same side of the street as Verrey's, though, of course, out of the range of McCarthy's vision. He had little doubt as to what, or rather who it was, gripping "Big Bill's" attention—the gangster, Mascagni. And as Withers remained where he was, it told McCarthy that Mascagni was hanging about somewhere in immediate proximity to the café.

"Do you often patronize this place, Baroness?" he asked with that engaging, white-toothed smile of his.

"Regularly," she told him. "I always take my *déjeuner* here. Nowhere else in London can I get the rolls and creamy Austrian coffee that I do here. From one o'clock, or a quarter past, to half-past two, my friends always know where to find me."

"And always in the same spot—this very pleasant window seat?" McCarthy asked.

She nodded. "Invariably. Luigi"—she nodded towards one of the elder waiters—"always keeps it for me; I am one of his regular patrons. I always have this table because I like to watch the people passing. I amuse myself wondering who and what they are, how they get a living, and all the rest of it."

"'Tis a grand sport," McCarthy murmured, his brain racing. "That is," he amended, "if you haven't to do that sort of thing for a living. Which reminds me," he said with a sigh, "that I have mine to earn, and sitting here in this delightful company won't do it. Someone has to roll the crime wave flat."

Bowing over the lady's hand, he moved towards the entrance, then turned as though a sudden thought had struck him. "Could I have one word with you, Sir William?"

Promptly Haynes got up and crossed to him. McCarthy led him still further out of any possible earshot of the lady at the table.

"Tell me, Bill," he asked quickly, "did the lady by any chance, before expressing a wish to make my acquaintance, happen to ask what case I was engaged upon?"

Haynes looked at him quickly. "Well, no, Mac," he said, a note of hesitation in his voice. "She didn't. That is, not specifically."

"And just what do you mean by 'not specifically'?" McCarthy asked.

"I mean that, so far as I can remember, she didn't ask any specific question about it," the A.C. answered. "I think it must have been myself that mentioned the fact that you were handling a most interesting murder which took place in Soho Square last night."

"I see," McCarthy said dryly. "And she was interested?"

"Oh, very; said she'd follow it with great interest in the newspapers."

"She pumped it out of you without you ever dreaming of it, y' dam' fool," was the thought in McCarthy's mind. What he actually said was: "It's nice to be appreciated, Bill. Y' didn't happen to mention anything of the…"

"The Whitehall business!" Sir William said, almost in a whisper. "Good God, no! There's no one breathing who could get a word of that out of me!"

"That's fine," McCarthy said, and took his departure.

Passing that window in the extreme corner of which the Baroness Eberhardt had her regular seat between the hours of one o'clock or a quarter-past to two-thirty daily, McCarthy tried to see if even his keen eyes could penetrate the wire blinds, but they could not; both the lady and Haynes were as invisible behind it as though it had been a brick wall.

"Yet she can see every soul that passes perfectly," he murmured to himself, that very definite knock upon the glass uppermost in his mind. "A queer mixture," he said puzzledly, as his eyes sought out Withers, to find him well down upon the other side of the road; "too queer to be probable."

Withers had very nearly arrived at Glasshouse Street before the inspector had caught him up.

"Mascagni," he said briefly, as McCarthy joined him. "Been tailin' him a bit. Just heard him tell someone that he'd be at Fasoli's to-night at about nine o'clock."

McCarthy nodded. "In which case, William, we'll defer any further chase of him for the time being. I also will be at Fasoli's. In the meantime I've got quite a lot of high-powered thinking to do, and one or two things to get ready before I crash that unspeakably dirty hole, the *Circolo Venezia* to-night. I think I'll walk home, exercising the fruitful mind as I go."

"Nothink else as I ca'n be a-doin' of, guv'nor?" Mr. Withers inquired. "Give it a name, sir, an' it's as good as done, as you know."

McCarthy thought for a moment. "Tell me," he asked suddenly, "is Mascagni still running around with that very beautiful lass, Tessa Domenico—that's if you follow the love affairs of Soho, Withers."

"Which I don't, I gi' y' my word, guv'nor," "Big Bill" informed him succinctly. "But as far as that there pair goes, I've seen 'em arahnd quite a bit, in restarongs and the flash dance places they go to. An' I've 'eard it said, by them as ought to know, that the reason as she's still a-goin' with 'im is that nobody else don't dare to look sideways at 'er. Arsting 'er to 'ave a dance is invitin' trouble, and as for takin' 'er aht—a bloke might as well go and get 'isself measured for 'is coffin, while Mascagni's about."

"That way, is it?" McCarthy said, with a shake of his head. "It's a queer world, Withers, and a sad one. We grow old in it and that's no good to anyone. You'd hardly believe it, but I've known Tessa Domenico, the Queen of Soho, as they call her, when she was a little kid toddling to school with a face smeared with jam—or maybe it was golden syrup. I remember her getting her first job—'twas as a waitress in Scarpetti's café in Oxford Street—and then she was what you might call all legs and wings. Then, she won that first prize in that beauty competition, and after that…never win a prize in a beauty competition, Withers; 'twill be the downfall of ye."

Mr. Withers grinned. "All the prizes I win wiv my clock, guv'nor, won't buy no property," he chuckled.

"You never can tell, Withers. I can remember little Tessa when you'd have said the same, and look at her now. I've been in the company of one very beautiful lady, but I'm bound to admit she has nothing on the kid that used to grab me by the hand and lead me to old Joe Anselmi's cart to buy her ice-cream. That was before he had the coffee-stall."

His face clouded at the memory of the harmless old man so wickedly done to death the night before; his mouth set into a thin hard line, which boded no good for the perpetrators of that terrible crime when, eventually, he clapped hands upon them.

"A rotten job that, sir," Withers said with a shake of his bull-head.

"Rotten!" McCarthy echoed. "Don't talk about it, Withers. The very thought of it makes me want to manhandle someone. You were asking just now if there was anything you could do. There is. At Verrey's there's a lady who will remain there until two-thirty—at any rate, that's her regular custom. She'll probably come out accompanied by Sir William Haynes. Park your car around the corner and keep an eye out for her. She lives in Grosvenor Square, and I want to know which particular house. In case she doesn't happen to be with Sir William, here's a description of her."

Rapidly he gave the taxi-man a verbal picture of the beautiful Baroness Lena Eberhardt so rich in detail that an artist might have painted a fairly decent portrait of that lady from it.

"Off you go, Withers, and, should she go home by a roundabout route make a special note of her contacts—as far as you're able, of course. Phone me to Dean Street with what information you've got, and by then I shall be able to know just how I can use you to-night. On your way, Withers; on your way!"

Chapter XIII

Withers Supplies Some Curious Information

In the seclusion of his own room McCarthy sat down to mull this thing out; to get it into some sort of chronological order which would give him fair ground to work from. The ghastly events of the night before, culminating as they did with the killing of Constable Harper, had unquestionably commenced with the brutal murder of the old coffee-stall man, Joe Anselmi. That that crime had been carefully premeditated by some cunning brain as the only method of getting the body of the intended victim out of Soho Square seemed to be an unarguable fact.

With regard to the second murder, there could be little or no doubt but that the killer must have been in possession of information that the *pseudo* Madame Rohner would go to those Soho Square offices at a given time last night, or, rather, early this morning. The possibility, indeed probability, was that Rohner had been decoyed there by some message which had to do with the plans stolen from Whitehall that afternoon.

That, again, argued that the killer, and those who he was connected with, knew not only of the existence of the plans and that they had been stolen by Rohner, but also that the thief was carrying them about, in all likelihood, preparatory to a speedy flight from the country with them. Which seemed to leave it as fairly beyond dispute that the thief was a secret-service agent of one country, while the killer was in the employ of another.

It seemed, to judge by the complete clearing out of Madame Rohner's office, that that mysterious personage had first made her way into the building and attended to the destruction of all traces of her (or, rather, "his") identity, or business, before coming in contact with the person, or, it might be, persons, who sought not only his life, but what he was known to be carrying. On the other hand, that clearance might have been made earlier in the evening and following the successful raid upon the safe in Whitehall. Whichever way it might have been, it made no appreciable difference. Of one thing McCarthy was quite certain, and that was that the room had not been cleared out by the murderer after the body of the victim had been got out of Soho Square in Anselmi's coffee-stall—the time lapse between the scream and the discovery of Harper's body was not sufficient to have permitted it being done.

To follow events along in their chronological order, the first person to claim his attention in the square had been that strange and, unquestionably sinister-looking person, the man with the ice-blue eyes. That, of course, might have been the merest coincidence and had nothing whatever to do with the murder. But, somehow, that "hunch" which he had followed at the time of the crime was as strong upon him now as it had been then; indeed, in the light of what had happened to Danny Regan, it had ceased in his opinion to be just one of those queer quirks of his brain which had so often led him in the right direction, but something far more tangible.

While the thought was uppermost in his mind he got up and phoned the mortuary. The D.S. was no longer there, but he had left a message with the mortuary-keeper for him. The blood scraped from Regan's clothing had, beyond any question of a doubt, come from the body on top of which the pickpocket had been pitched on the floor of the car that had taken him to Hampstead Heath. So much for that. And, in connection with the removal of that body from Soho Square, it struck the inspector how large a part luck played in his particular game. Had it not been for that outbreak of fire which had lit the totally blacked-out Soho Square, it was a thousand to one that the passage out of it of Joe Anselmi's coffee-stall would ever have been seen, and the murder of the old man never have been connected with the Soho Square case in a lifetime. Both that crime and the method of transposal of the body from Soho Square would in all probability have gone down on the records as "insoluble mysteries."

There seemed to be little question—none whatever in McCarthy's mind, though he had not one scintilla of evidence to support it—that the man with the ice-blue eyes had communicated to some, pre-arranged point from the telephone-booth in Marylebone Lane, and given the information to confederates he was being shadowed, made a rendezvous to pick him up in Park Lane, and thus trouble had fallen hard upon Regan's head.

And then on top of all this had come that most amazing *rencontre* with the Baroness Lena Eberhardt that morning! There, indeed, was an extraordinary coincidence if ever one had happened in his strangely varied professional experience, and brought about by no less a person than the A.C., at that. Almost, the first name which had passed the lips of this Austrian aristocrat had been that of the woman who was no woman, and most certainly was a daring, and extraordinarily skilful, secret-service agent. Whatever else was wrapped in mystery that much at any rate had been proved without doubt.

And yet the very casualness with which the name had been introduced, even though coupled with the fact that the baroness had specifically stated that she had communicated that morning with the person who at that time was lying upon a slab in the mortuary, left McCarthy in a welter of doubts. Could it be that there was another person of the same name, a professional clairvoyant, crystal-gazer, or palmist, in existence in London? The woman had mentioned no address or even locality, but she had specifically said that she had telephoned her, and the fact that there was only one Madame Rohner in the telephone-directory, and that the one in Soho Square, could not be got over.

Nor did any doubt exist that she knew that he was the officer in charge of the Soho Square case; whether Bill Haynes had volunteered the information without realizing it, or she had skilfully pumped it out of him made no difference; the point was that she knew it. The thing exercising his mind was: had that name been mentioned in all innocence, or, as he had suspected, in Verrey's, been put out simply as a lead to extract information from him she could not possibly have asked for—without implicating herself, if only in the most indirect manner? It was a bit of a twister, he told himself; looked at from any angle the mention of that name opened up quite a field for investigation. And, it would *get* it! It was just possible, if the woman made any contacts after leaving Verrey's, that Withers might be able to pick up a lead that would prove helpful.

But the only personal lead he had was the attempt to run him down on his way back from the mortuary that morning; the very deliberate effort made by the driver of that car to rub him out, finally, not a couple of hundred yards from his own doorstep. That car must have trailed him, and cleverly, at that, from the very mortuary door, keeping out of sight until the chance came for the final rush. Why? And there again was a certain fly in the ointment, in as much that he was in company with Danny Regan—had it been Daniel's light which it had been intended to blot out permanently? It was quite possible though, in his opinion, not very probable, particularly in the circumstances.

That the underworld repaid their grudges in bloodthirsty fashion, and did not stop at either crippling, complete maiming, or even murder in the process was no news to him, but that any of them, no matter how big the vendetta, would have attempted it openly, and also under the very eyes of the one Scotland Yard man who the denizens of Soho held in something more than respect, was a thing that he could not credit. Had Danny Regan been found with a knife in his chest, or, still more likely, driven through his back, it would have been understandable enough, but an attempt to bump him off, not only in broad daylight and in the presence of witnesses, but also in the actual company of Detective Inspector McCarthy was too incredible for belief. No, Danny was not the one picked out for elimination.

And, gang-boss Flo. Mascagni had been in the attempt! That Mascagni, despite the fact that from time to time he had sold information of his fellows (and possibly *because* of that very fact) would have been glad to see *finis* written to the book of McCarthy, the inspector did not doubt for a moment. But, and this McCarthy knew equally well, Mascagni would not have been in at the job, personally, for a thousand pounds, if he could have helped himself. Yet, despite his best efforts to remain unseen, Mascagni *had* been there, had been recognized by men who knew him and were not likely to make any mistake, and that told McCarthy that

Mascagni must be under the thumb, and stand in terror of, someone considerably bigger than himself. Who?

Mascagni was his mark to follow, right enough, but, by an extremely devious route which would never be suspected by the tricky Italian. Like most of his kind he was as cunning as a rat, and, notwithstanding the fact that he had his full share of the abject cowardice of a gangster when tackled single-handed, McCarthy knew that even if he had him rushed straight into a police-station for interrogation he would get nothing out of him. The unwritten law of the underworld is a still tongue, and woe betide the one who breaks that law! All the police can do to him is as nothing to what will happen later, at the hands of his fellows.

McCarthy's mind turned again upon that extraordinarily beautiful creature, Tessa Domenico. So she and the vicious Floriello were still running in company, according to Bill Withers; information which had rather surprised him, for when he had last seen the glorious-looking Tessa she had been moving in much higher, though still rather raffish company. She was, to use a term not altogether confined to the underworld, "in the big money."

And certainly in the place in which he had seen her—an extremely select, if not altogether exclusive dance-club—she had been the cynosure of all eyes and, he had admitted freely, had been well worthy of the attention she claimed.

She was tall, dark, and olive-skinned, with the soft, velvety colouring of the Italian race, and her features were absolutely flawless—perfection itself. She gowned in a style which would have made her mother and father stare in utter incredulousness. No cheap and showy stuff, hers, from a bargain counter, but the creations of an artist in clothes.

Had those connoisseurs of a female perfection which had instantly aroused the unstinted admiration of all men present, and the equally unstinted envy of the women, been informed that the woman whose beauty their eyes feasted upon was a child of the gutters of Soho and the affianced bride of a flash gangster, they would, in all probability, have said without hesitation that their informant was mad; that such beauty could only have been allied with the bluest of blue blood. Yet, according to Withers, it was true enough, and it certainly *had* been so, of McCarthy's own knowledge.

The love affairs of Soho were an open book to him, if only from the very simple reason that the greater part of its crime sprang directly from them. He found himself wondering cynically just how much love there was upon the girl's side in that arrangement, and how much of it was fear of the razor-like steel blade, or automatic pistol, Floriello Mascagni would use with remarkable speed upon any persistent rival for her affections—and possibly herself as well. It was a nice point.

He was still considering it when his telephone bell rang. Lifting the receiver the bull-like tones of Mr. William Withers assailed his ears.

"It's me, guv'nor," he informed McCarthy, somewhat unnecessarily.

"So I hear, Withers," the inspector returned dryly, "'The voice that breathed,' and all that. Any luck?"

A note of dubiousness promptly entered into the taxi-man's voice.

"That all depends as the way that y' look at it, guv'nor," he replied. "Any'ow, 'ere's what 'appened. She come out of Verrey's and 'is 'Igh…I mean Sir William, was wiv 'er, like you said. F'r a minnit I thought 'e'd spotted me and was goin' to call me up, but 'e didn't. He shakes 'ands wiv 'er, and goes off along Regent Street towards Piccadilly. She crossed the road to Liberty's corner and stands lookin' at the winders for a bit. She kep' a-lookin' arter 'im now and agin, and then she 'ails a taxi, and…"

"Just a minute, Withers. She kept looking after Sir William, you say? Did it strike you, by any chance, that she might have been keeping an eye on him to see that he really was well out of her way?"

"Well, sir, in a sort of a kind of a way, that's jest wot I did think. Any'ow, she gits in this taxi, and turns east at Oxford Street as far as Charing Cross Road. Then she turns into Soho Square and goes right round it, slow-like, and out agin by Greek Street."

"Didn't stop anywhere at all?" McCarthy asked, perplexedly.

"No, guv'nor, she never stopped nowhere. She goes down Greek Street like I said, then turns into Dean Street. At a tobacconists, just a bit above your crib and on the other side of the street, she pulls up and goes in. That German bloke's place; Kirchner, I think the name is."

"Go on, Withers," McCarthy encouraged. "This is very interesting."

"She musta bought some cigarettes, or summink there, becos when she come out she 'ad a packet in 'er 'and. Afore she gets back into the taxi I see 'er givin' your place a real once over—if you'd 'appened to 'a' bin lookin' aht of the winder, you couldn't 'a' 'elped seein' 'er. Then off she goes round agin into Greek Street—and that's where I lost 'er."

"Lost her," McCarthy echoed.

"Yus, guv'nor, she gimme the shake right enough; no good sayin' anythink else."

"Just at what point did you lose her, Withers?" McCarthy asked puzzledly. For anyone to give "Big Bill" Withers the slip in Soho meant that they knew that cosmopolitan portion of the metropolis thoroughly; no-one not thoroughly acquainted with its many alleys and short cuts, generally, could have possibly accomplished it. "For a lady who resides in Grosvenor Square and is one of the elect, that's rather unusual isn't it, Withers?"

"I'll say it is, sir," that worthy returned somewhat ruefully. "I'd 'ave bet a hundred nikker to a bar of tuppeny soap that it couldn't 'ave been did, but it was."

"Where was it?" McCarthy asked again.

"It was quite near Fasoli's joint," "Big Bill" informed him. "There was a bit of a jam, as was caused by one o' Gatti's ice-carts a-gettin' blocked by a council cart. A rozzer 'ops in and starts muckin' abaht straight'nin' things aht, and 'e 'olds me back a minnit. 'Er taxi cuts through t'wards Frith Street an' as soon as I can I get's arter it and catch it up. Then I see as it's empty. She musta paid 'im off and slipped off while this 'ere ice-cart was blockin' my view. It 'appened to be a bloke as I don't know as was drivin', a new 'un, and cocky. When I arsts 'im where he dropped 'is fare, 'e wants to know what th' 'ell it's got to do wiv me. If I 'adn't a been on a job for you I'd a shown 'im quick and lively. 'Owever, there it was, guv'nor, I'd lost 'er right enough, an' although I cruises rahnd two or three times, I never got sight of 'er again."

"An exceedingly queer business altogether, Withers," the inspector commented thoughtfully. "At Fasoli's corner, you say? She couldn't have nipped in there by any chance, I suppose, ridiculous as the idea may seem?"

"She couldn't 'ave, guv'nor," Mr. Withers responded earnestly. "Fasoli's door was shut tight, bein' arter 'ours by that time, an' I took a good 'ard look all round there, but there were no signs of 'er."

"Well," McCarthy said philosophically, "it can't be helped, Withers; these little things will happen. Get home now, and stand by for a ring from me at about nine o'clock to-night. That's all."

But for some time after he had rung off McCarthy paced his room, deep in thought. Quite a number of things in

Withers' report were intriguing him greatly, and not the least of them was the attention the lady had given to his own domicile. That, and the fact that she had so skilfully eluded Withers in the very heart of Soho wanted quite a bit of thinking out—for a lady of her social status. So, also, did that curious tap upon the window at Verrey's, unquestionably made by the fingers of Signor Floriello Mascagni.

Chapter XIV

At the Circolo Venezia

That extremely unpleasant-looking person, the Signor Luigi Fasoli, had but an hour or so opened the doors of what was quite easily the dirtiest wine-shop in Soho, for all that it was glorified by the grandiloquent name of the *Circolo Venezia*.

The place itself consisted of a long, exceedingly dirty bar which opened from the street, along which was set a built-in wooden bench with a few tables in front of it. On the other side there was a counter, behind which were huge barrels of the vilest red, or white, poison ever sold to man as wine.

Behind this, and entered by two swing doors, was another very large and dirty room which contained a billiards table and a number of smaller tables at which the clientele who patronized that particular place played cards, or dominoes, or other games of skill, or chance, favoured by the younger school of London-born Italians.

That clientele was divided into three entirely different classes. The first the elders of Soho of the rougher type, who lined the bar and long bench-seat of the front compartment, and among which—as Scotland Yard well knew—were numbered several members of those dread societies, the *Camorrista*, and the Sicilian *Mafia*. Sinister-looking personages, these, about whom grim stories were whispered among their fellows.

The second group was composed of a number of Germans—mostly restaurant workers—who had been deprived of their usual rendezvous when a certain notorious Bismarck Club had been raided and closed. These kept very much to themselves, and, despite the wavering Axis, were not over popular with the Latin patrons of the *Circolo Venezia*.

The third and largest group of all frequented, and over-ran generally, the inner and much larger room generally known as the "club." They were of the flashy type of young Soho-born Italians who, for the greater part, earned the daily crust infesting the courses where such war-time racing as there was took place by day, and the third-class West End restaurants and dance-halls, by night. Sleek, oily and over-dressed, wicked rats in the "mob" but arrant curs single-handed, they formed, really, the bulk of Fasoli's customers. They were headed by, and gave implicit obedience to, that extremely good-looking personage, in a well-oiled, raffish and over-jewelled way, Floriello Mascagni.

It was this gentleman who, shortly after seven o'clock passed through the front double-doors of Fasoli's wine shop, and gave its ill-favoured proprietor a hard, but meaning look.

"Nothing yet," Fasoli said, in an underbreath. "Da lady has-a been here dis afternoon," he went on, through lips that never moved. "She says a that *he* will-a be here to-night, later, and you are to wait for him. He will-a ring som'time dis evening."

Mascagni nodded. "Okay," he returned, in the same still-mouthed way.

"You weel-a find som' of da boys inside," he said, aloud. "Dey just-a com' back from Cheltenham."

Passing through into the inner room, Mascagni beckoned to one huge hulking brute who was playing pool, and whose face was disfigured by a knife-slash which ran right across it. Promptly he put down his cue and came across to the small table at which Mascagni had seated himself.

Taking from an inner pocket a thick roll of Treasury notes, he pushed them across to Mascagni.

"'Protection money,'" he said gruffly. "Not too good—the books went down badly on the first three races."

Taking up the notes—Mascagni's soft Italian eyes had gone as hard as two agates at the sight of the money—he thumbed them over with the swiftness of long practice, then swore softly in Italian.

"Rotten!" he commented. "I shall have to gyp things up on that course."

Taking ten one-pound notes, he pushed them across the table and stuffed the rest in his breast-pocket.

"What else?" he asked sharply.

From a wash-leather bag the other poured out upon the table a collection of jewellery, for the greater part tie-pins of somewhat lurid design though the stones were good enough, and three heavy gold watches and chains.

"That's the pickings for the day, Flo," he was told.

Mascagni sorted them over with a finger, then nodded to his henchman to replace them.

"You know where to take them," he said curtly. "And don't let the old swine do you the way he did with the last lot. If he tries it, tell him we'll put a fire-stick into his place, and pick a time when we know he's in bed! Go on—get about it!"

Four amongst those present he beckoned over to him, and to each passed some money from the roll. They were the working gang who had been out at the racecourse "levying" that afternoon.

This business transacted, Mascagni sat on in brooding thought for a while. It was plainly evident that he was ill at ease and, indeed, as nervy as a cat. After a while he rang a bell upon the table, which Fasoli hurriedly answered.

"Get the boys a drink," he ordered abruptly, "and bring me something. But not that rot-gut that you sell out there. No word yet?" he asked quickly, and in the same undertone in which he had first inquired.

Fasoli shook his unkempt head.

"Notta yet," he said in the same tone. "Any time-a now I expec'."

"Everything O.K. out there?" Mascagni asked, as a quick, excited jabber of conversation went up in the outer bar.

Fasoli shrugged his shoulders.

"Ever't'ing all right," he said. "Just-a that hell-hound, Vanadi, he com' in. Always a noise when 'e com'."

"The first thing you know he'll start a fight and you'll have the cops in on you," Mascagni growled. "Why do you stand him here at all? He only turns up about once every six months, and it's a police job every time he does come."

"He spenda plentee money," Fasoli answered. "Spenda more in two, t'ree hours than alla da rest put together."

"He'll lose you your licence, one day," Mascagni said. "Anyhow, keep him out of this room. He mauled one of my mob so badly last time that he was in the hospital three weeks. He'll get what's coming to him one of these nights."

Fasoli gave a quick glance back towards the bar, as if terrified that the customer in question might hear and promptly start something which would not be finished in a hurry.

Signor Paolo Vanadi was, without any question, the most quarrelsome person who ever paid occasional, though fairly regular, visits to Soho, there to drink inordinate quantities of the wines of his native land. Where he came from no-one actually knew, though some said from the north of England, where he was supposed to be in the wholesale ice-cream trade. But upon these visits he spent money like water, comparatively speaking, and invariably drank himself into a state of sullen ferocity which, sooner or later burst like a volcano. He was an inveterate fighter and, moreover, could get on with it like a professional boxer.

Upon more than one occasion, he had fallen foul of Mascagni's gangsters, and what he had done to such of them as had jointly and severally tackled him was little less than a crime.

"You notta talk that way, Flo," Fasoli said uneasily. "Vanadi a *Camorrista* man. You notta can tell wit' them. Getta foul of them, and plenty of trouble eet com'."

It was quite evident in the expression which flitted across Mascagni's olive-skinned face that the mere mention of that brotherhood had very deep and significant meaning for him.

"I don't want any trouble with him," he said. "All I want you to do is to keep him out of here."

It was, perhaps, five minutes later, and in the interim the sounds denoting that Signor Vanadi was getting to his usual state of belligerent drunkenness were increasing, that Fasoli put his head around the door and gave the gangster a meaning look. Instantly Mascagni got up and moved towards another door which all who frequented the place knew led to Fasoli's private apartments upstairs.

Scarcely had he turned towards it when the double-doors opened and the talked-of Vanadi lurched a foot or two into the room and stood glaring around him with unconcealed contempt.

"There we all are," he said in Italian, and with a twisted smile at his mouth. "All the little rats in their sewer! One day some honest citizen will come in and clean the whole lot of them up for the dirt they are!"

Not a word came from any of the mob around the billiards table.

"Hallo, Vanadi," Mascagni greeted with as much affability as he could in the attempt to ward off trouble.

"And there talks the King-rat!" the gentleman addressed spat, looking for the moment as though he were about to move in Mascagni's direction.

Inwardly cursing bitterly, though outwardly he showed nothing but a smile, Mascagni hurried to the door and departed through it. For a full minute Vanadi stood and glared at the others in unmistakable invitation for them to start something. But as not one of them moved so much as a muscle, he spat upon the floor contemptuously and lurched out into the front bar again.

Hurrying upstairs, Mascagni picked up the receiver Fasoli had left off for him, but first he saw that the two doors into the room were closed tightly.

"Hallo?" he said in a scarcely audible voice.

"Mascagni?" came across the line sharply.

"That's me, Boss," he said quickly.

"That package which was passed to you in Soho Square last night," the voice went on in the same peremptory manner, and speaking perfect English with just the very faintest touch of Northern German accent. "You have it with you?"

"No," Mascagni answered promptly. "After what happened in the square last night, I reckoned it safer not to have it on me. I got Luigi to plant it down...you know where. If the cops knew what it was and were hunting for it, I didn't want it found on *me*, if anything went wrong."

"And what is there that that great brain of yours thinks might go wrong, as far as you are concerned?" the other questioned, open contempt in his voice.

Mascagni ground his teeth in silent rage; it took him all his time to keep that emotion out of his voice. "This," he answered. "How do I know that I was not spotted when you tried to do McCarthy in this morning? I don't think I was, but you never can tell with him; he gets to work in some dam' queer ways when he starts, as we've reason for knowing in Soho. But suppose he had seen me and within an hour or two I'd been picked up by the police? Would it have been all right if I'd had that stuff you took off the woman in the square last night?"

"*Gott in Himmel!*" burst from the other. "Are you a fool altogether to speak like that over the telephone! You know that it would not. Perhaps," he conceded, though ungraciously, "you were right not to carry it with you. Tell Fasoli that I shall come for the packet to-night at about eleven o'clock."

"You wanted me to stand by for orders, didn't you?" Mascagni growled.

"I still do," came back the sharp answer. "Though as far as that is concerned I can give them to you now. I want you…"

"Just a minute," Mascagni interrupted. "I've got a date for to-night—an important date. Can't somebody else take on this job? I've got plenty of good men here that can be trusted…"

"Doubtless quite as much as you can be yourself," came icily from the other. "But I want you to do this work, Mascagni; *you*, and you alone." The icy note gave place to an imperative one. "Those are my orders, you understand? *Orders!* I do not brook any argument concerning them."

The hot red blood surged up under Mascagni's olive skin, but he held himself in check.

"Do not forget, my friend," the voice went on, coldly menacing, "that you are as much involved in what happened last night, as anyone else. You and your men removed the first obstacle in our path, and brought that coffee-stall along when the second obstacle was eliminated. You also it was who took a certain something and also that fool who followed me to the place where it—and he, were found. It was for that reason that I insisted upon you, personally, being in the car this morning when a certain attempt was made to remove yet another. Keep that in your mind, Mascagni, and also something else: that the first moment you make any move, or disobey any order which I conceive to be necessary for the success of my projects there will be another, and an extremely speedy elimination. I leave you to guess who that will be."

So sinister was the tone in which these words were uttered that whatever urge to open defiance the gang-boss had in him speedily ebbed away, to give place to something remarkably like fear. Utterly merciless as he could be towards those of his kind who incurred his displeasure amongst the denizens of the underworld, he had seen enough of the methods of the man now ordering him about like a dog to instil in him a wholesome terror of bringing his wrath down upon himself, personally. The sight he had witnessed in Soho Square had not been a pretty one; he had no wish for the scene to be repeated, with himself as one of the two principal actors in it.

"Oh, all right, all right," he snapped quickly. "Let's have the orders. I can put the date off."

"I should," came back to him in amazingly equable tones. "Since I saw you this morning certain information has come to me that this McCarthy is putting forth his very best efforts to clear up the mystery of the Soho Square death. Whether he has any knowledge of the cause of that unfortunate decease—the packet, which we will merely say you know of—I cannot tell. Nor have I any certain knowledge as to whether the identity of that person has been discovered yet. That is a matter of considerable importance to me, and I want you to get out at once, pick up the track of McCarthy and watch his movements closely. It may be that some act of his may reveal what I want to know. Set about that business at once and it may be that you will be able to report something useful to me at eleven o'clock. That is all."

"But I haven't the faintest idea where to pick McCarthy up," Mascagni protested. "He's like a blasted jumping-jack; here, there, and everywhere."

"That is your business," the other informed him coldly. "You will prosecute it to the very utmost of your ability—if you are wise. Until eleven o'clock."

There was no more. Flo. Mascagni could hear the other hang up his receiver, then the line went dead. Returning to the club room, he picked three of the older men of his gang, tough-looking specimens, who, he knew, could be depended upon to not only use cunning, but could put up a real fight if necessary.

"The rest of you clear out of here sharp at closing time and make yourselves scarce."

For a moment or two he stood thinking, then slipping upstairs again to the telephone, dialled a certain number. A low, seductive female voice answered his call.

"Who is it?" she asked.

"It's me—Flo.," he told her. "I can't take you out dancing to-night as I promised, Tessa. He's found me a job to do, dam' him."

"He? Who?" she asked, but without exhibiting the disappointment in her voice that he had expected to hear.

"The Big Shot. The one I told you about who's been finding the big dough lately."

"The one whose name you don't know?" she asked.

"I know the name he's travelling under," he answered. "But it's not his real one. The swine is a German. Don't talk about him, he seems to have ears that reach everywhere!" he added viciously.

"You sound as if you don't like him, Flo.," she said.

A wicked laugh came from Mascagni.

"Like him! I like him so much that if I could see a chiv in his throat I'd laugh for a fortnight! But I want his dough,

Tessa, and he's bad medicine to fall out with. But one of these days I'll show him something that he won't forget in a hurry."

"Why?" she asked laconically.

"Why?" he echoed. "Because he thinks he's everything and the rest don't matter! Gives his orders as if you were a dog, and his threats at the same time. I suppose I've got to stick him while I want him, but one of the best days I'll ever know will be the one when I'll either see him dead or with handcuffs on. And one will be about the same as the other."

A low, musical laugh came to him over the line.

"You love him not, Flo.," she said.

"I love him not!" Mascagni answered grimly. "And one day he'll know it. Well, I've got to get going. I'll phone you to-morrow."

"Leave it till the evening, Flo.," she said. "I shall be free then."

"What do you mean by 'free then'?" he asked jealously. "What are you doing the rest of the day?"

But no answer came to him, and for the second time that evening he heard the receiver hung up on him. He was still muttering curses when he joined the three he had selected for the night's work and left the *Circolo Venezia*.

As he passed through the outer bar the wild-looking Signor Paolo Vanadi was holding forth luridly upon some subject or other. Pausing for a moment to throw one contemptuous stare at the quartette as they went through, he jerked a thumb towards them.

"Rats!" he observed, that all might hear. "Rats on two legs instead of four! The only difference is that the four-legged ones have more courage!"

Receiving no answer of any sort of kind to this jibe, he spat deliberately upon the highly-polished shoes of the gangster bringing up the rear, then went on with his impassioned harangue.

Chapter XV

The Packet Changes Hands

At five to eleven to the minute, Fasoli cleared his place, then closed and barred the front doors of the *Circolo Venezia*. His unusual earliness brought savage expostulations from some of his patrons, of which he took no notice whatever. Strangely enough, the one he had expected most trouble with, Paolo Vanadi, he had none at all, for at about the time he commenced picking up the dirty glasses, that gentleman, having drunk himself into an almost lunatic state, simply disappeared.

Having closed, Fasoli did not hang around his bar cleaning up as usual, but got to that upstairs room, and sat waiting by the telephone. At two minutes to eleven it rang. The same cold voice which had addressed Mascagni earlier in the evening came to his ears.

"I shall be there, at the rear door, in precisely three minutes," it informed him. "Have the packet ready that Mascagni handed over to you for safekeeping to-day. I have no wish to stay there longer than is necessary. Is Mascagni there?"

"No, signor, but I expect-a heem ever-a minute. Eet ees notta eleven yet, signor. Mascagni good-a boy," he observed, almost timidly. "Somet'ing onexpec' keep-a heem late. Trust Flo. to carry-a da orders out."

The words were hardly out of his mouth when there came a peculiar, low-noted whistle from the back yard.

"Mascagni ees 'ere now—signor. I 'ear hees wheestl—a."

Putting back the receiver he hurried to the back door, unlocked it, and opened it cautiously. Mascagni entered alone.

"He 'as just-a rung up," Fasoli informed him. "Weel be-a 'ere in two, t'ree minutes."

"The best I wish him is that he'll break his bloody neck getting here," Mascagni growled. "He's after the packet— you'd better have it ready. His Highness doesn't like being kept waiting—blast him."

Fasoli glanced at him queerly, and for a second looked as though he was about to make some observation. But evidently he thought better of it and made again for his back door.

"Lock eet after me," he requested. "And open up when he com'."

Outside his door he listened while Mascagni shot the bolts. Suddenly, but at some distance away, there rose upon the still night air the sound of a fierce brawl, topped by altercation in a high-pitched hysterical voice. With a certain amount of relief Fasoli recognized the voice—it was that madman, Paolo Vanadi, fallen foul of the police again! Had it not been for the money he spent so liberally during his periodical visits, Fasoli could have wished that he could have remained in their hands for the rest of his existence. The brawl was still at its height as he made his way across a small yard which would have been a veritable deathtrap to any stranger who had endeavoured to negotiate it in this inky blackness, but the wine-shop keeper passed with the utmost certainty through the obstacles towards a ramshackle shed which stood in a corner of the yard. Into this he disappeared, and as he did so the sound of the faraway brawl ended with a suddenness which suggested that the unruly Vanadi had been laid low at last—possibly with a police truncheon.

Scarcely had Fasoli disappeared than a back gate which led into an alley was opened cautiously, and two other persons entered the yard. The one who led the way must have had the eyes of a cat to avoid accident, or else, like Fasoli, was so well acquainted with the place that he could cross it blindfold. A moment later he tapped in a peculiar way upon the door; without hesitation Mascagni unlocked and opened.

The first person to enter would have been promptly recognized by Inspector McCarthy, even by such portion of his face as could be seen, as the man who had supped in Signora Spadoglia's the night before—the one he had mentally christened, and thought of, as the "man with the ice-blue eyes." At the present moment those strange-looking members were not so much the colour of ice as of chilled steel. He was garbed in totally different fashion to the night before, wearing rough tweeds and a heavy overcoat of the same material, the collar of which was turned up to his ears. The soft felt hat which topped the lot was snapped down in front to cover those strange eyes, but the moment he entered the room he pushed it back clear of them and fixed Mascagni with a stare so steady that it seemed peculiarly malevolent in its intensity.

But it was the person who accompanied and, by the way, the one who had led the way across the case- and cask-strewn yard, who was certainly the most noticeable of the two at that moment. He was, literally, a dwarf of certainly not more than four feet high, but with the shoulder-spread of a man two feet taller. To add to the queerness, indeed unnaturalness, of his appearance, his head and hands would have been in proper proportion upon a man of the latter height, yet his feet were tiny.

He was dressed in a chauffeur's uniform of dark grey, and carried a pair of leather gauntlets in his left hand. In features he was as repulsive as even a man of his unusual proportions could be. The whole of his face was heavily pock-marked, while his nose was of that natural order of snub which appears to have no bridge whatever, and just juts from the face in one wide-nostrilled point. His ears were huge and splayed out at right angles to his face, while his mouth, for sheer cruelty, would have done justice to a man-eating shark. The moment he had knocked upon the door and Mascagni had opened it, he dropped back behind the man who was apparently his master, and effaced himself in a corner by the door.

"Well," the newcomer asked, in that abrupt, harsh voice which seemed natural to him, "have you anything to report?"

Mascagni shook his head sullenly.

"No," he answered. "I and three of my men have hunted everywhere I could think of to pick up traces of him, but we've had no luck. He's not in Soho to-night, that I'm certain of."

"He was in the West End at two o'clock today," the other said frowningly. "That I know for positive fact."

In the same sullen way Mascagni shrugged his shoulders. "He may be still for all I know," he returned. "All I've got to say is that I've hunted Soho for him, and can't find him, nor have I struck anyone who's seen him to-night. I might have gone on further, only you wanted me here at eleven o'clock, and it takes time to go the rounds."

There was a certain note of surly defiance in the Soho-Italian's voice as he spoke; a note which the other was not slow to pick up. The steely light in the pale eyes intensified ever so slightly, though by no other sign did he show annoyance or, for the matter of that, interest.

"Perhaps I am wrong," he said quietly, and, indeed, amiably, "but you sound somewhat disgruntled, Mascagni?"

The tone in which the words were spoken gave the gangster courage to get something off his chest which had lain dormant there ever since his projected programme with Tessa Domenico had been upset by this man's peremptory orders.

"If that means that I'm sore, you can take it as right," he spat, his native viciousness showing for the first time to the man who watched him with that unblinking stare. "It's all dam' fine you ordering this and that, and speaking to me as if I were some dog in the gutter. But don't forget one thing…"

"And what is that?" the other interrupted, in a strangely quiet voice.

"That it wasn't me who killed the woman in Soho Square last night—it's not me McCarthy's after."

"No?"

"No! You can tell me that I had a cut in it as much as you like, and my answer to that is that I knew nothing about it until I saw it done, and if I had known, I wouldn't have been where I was. You can bet on that."

"What is the difference, in so far as the law is concerned, between one murder and another?" the man with the icy eyes queried almost pleasantly. "Who killed the owner of the coffee-stall?"

"Not me," Mascagni snapped quickly. "I wasn't mug enough for that."

"I think that if ever you stand in the dock for complicity in either charge, the mere fact that you did not actually commit the murders with your own hands will not stand you in very good stead. You are an accessory, as the English law puts it, both before and after both crimes."

Mascagni scowled. "When I stand in the dock for it," he snarled, "you can bet every penny you've got that you'll be there with me. Take that from me."

"*Ach*, so? That is the way of it, is it?" The speaker moved with a long gliding stride towards Mascagni, who promptly backed away from him and dropped his hand into his right coat pocket. "Be warned, fool, do not attempt to pull that weapon you have there if you value your own worthless and useless existence. To repeat your own phrase, you can take it from me that you would be a dead man, before you could as much as point it. You will be well advised to remove that hand before—before something extremely unpleasant happens to you."

One quick look Mascagni took into those unmoving eyes, then slowly his hand came out of the pocket—empty.

"That is better, much better. Now, you listen to me. The first movement that you make in any direction, which I consider inimical to either myself or my plans, will be your last. That you are too big a cur to ever whisper a word that might land you where you should have been long ago, in a felon's dock, I am perfectly certain. However, here and now I give you fair warning, which is something I do not generally trouble myself to do where rats of your breed are concerned. Make one false step—and you know the consequences."

A tap, the same peculiar knock as that which had admitted them, came upon the door.

"Open it, Ludwig," he ordered curtly.

Without a word the dwarf did so, and Fasoli hurried into the room and quickly closed and bolted the door after himself. One quick glance he shot at the two standing there, then took a flat, oilskin-wrapped packet from the inside of his shirt, and handed it over.

"What you wanted, signor," he said, utter subservience in his voice.

"I wrap eet in-a da piece oilskin," he said fawningly. "Eet damp—da blue colour she com' off onna da fingers."

"Thanks." Carefully and deliberately the man with the icy eyes unwrapped the oilskin and examined the contents, then as carefully rewrapped it and placed it in his breast-pocket. From a notecase he took two wads of treasury notes, the smaller of which he handed to Fasoli, whose eyes gleamed at the sight of the money.

"I t'ank you, signor; I t'ank you," the wine-shop keeper almost grovelled, clutching at the notes.

The second packet he flung upon the floor at Mascagni's feet. "The pay you were promised," he said coldly. "Let it remind you, Mascagni, of a very important fact: that I *keep* my promises—pleasant, and unpleasant." He made an abrupt gesture towards the door. "Get out," he ordered curtly. "Get out—before I change my mind as to the method of dealing with you."

Without a word Mascagni picked up the packet of notes, and thrust them in his pocket, then crossed to the door, avoiding the glare in the eyes of the other. Fasoli, scenting the imminence of stark tragedy, opened the door hurriedly, and Mascagni slouched through it without a word. Five minutes later his other guests left, and, it was with a sigh of intense relief that he locked and bolted the door, for the last time he hoped, that night.

"*Madonna mia!*" he muttered, as the last sound of their departure reached him from the yard. "I do not like that one! I am afraid of heem."

It was as the pair moved stealthily along in the blackness of the alley at the rear of Fasoli's that the icy-eyed man spoke again.

"I will drive the car home, Ludwig," he said quietly. "I think it will be wiser for you to do a little job to-night, and not risk leaving it till later. A job," he added, "which is one after your own heart. You understand?"

"*Ja*, Herr Baron," the dwarf chuckled. "One after my own heart, indeed!"

A moment later, he had disappeared into the impenetrable gloom which was Greek Street in the black-out.

His master kept along towards Oxford Street at a pace which suggested that those strange eyes of his had something of the feline power of seeing in the dark in them. Only once he paused as though he heard some movement not far away from him, stood listening a moment, then went on again.

As he did so someone, moving with the stealth of a creature of the wild, kept a little behind him upon the other side of the road, though certain it was that if his game was shadowing, he could have seen nothing of his quarry. At one corner this unseen second person stopped as though in a quandary, then felt his way into a narrow alley which ran from Greek Street towards the rear of its business premises. A second later he had barely time to flatten himself against the wall when a car shot along the alley without lights of any sort, its mudguards almost brushing against him. It turned into Greek Street, and before the shadower could get to the corner its lights were switched on after it swung again into Oxford Street, running in an easterly direction. But one light was not on—that which should have illumined, even if ever so faintly, the rear number plate.

"Lost him," the shadower exclaimed ruefully. "I should have been prepared for something of this sort."

Chapter XVI

Exit Floriello Mascagni!

Floriello Mascagni, so summarily dismissed from the *Circolo Venezia*, landed out into the streets again in a condition of white-hot rage. Not a little of that violent emotion was caused by the fact of the poor showing he knew himself to have made in front of a man he despised, Luigi Fasoli. He, himself, had invariably treated the wine-shop keeper with unconcealed contempt; the contempt of a gang-boss whose mob would have wrecked the place without turning a hair if the older man had dared to show any open resentment. If he knew his Fasoli, the whisper that Flo. Mascagni had taken a verbal trouncing without as much as lifting a finger, would be well around Soho before he was so much older.

His rage was further aggravated by the thought that, but for this German swine's autocratic orders to meet, and report, to him there at eleven o'clock, he would have been dancing, or otherwise enjoying himself, with Tessa. A moment's reflection upon this point brought him realization that, when all was said and done, it was but a little after eleven o'clock now—quite time enough for them to enjoy an hour or two at one or two of the underworld dance dives where he and his kind were especially catered for, and where closing hours were an extremely elastic business.

Making for the nearest telephone-booth he dialled her lodgings in Doughty Street—Tessa had months ago left the home circle for brighter surroundings: the simple ways of Giacomo Domenico, the wine-cask maker, and his wife, Lucia, were not hers, these days.

His ring was answered by her landlady, who informed him that Tessa had gone out an hour or so ago, and had evidently gone to some restaurant or night club since she had arrayed herself in her latest finery. She had left no word, either as to where she was going, or as to what time she might be expected to return.

A quick stab of jealousy aggravated still further the savage passions already burning in his breast. Knowing her, it was not feasible that she had dressed in that style to spend what was left of the night by herself. Who, then, had she gone to meet?

He prowled the streets for a while, then decided to put in an hour or two at a certain club frequented by gamblers, which also had the convenient tab "Circolo" tacked on to it for obvious reasons—this particular dive was glorified by the title of the *Circolo Romagna*, though the Romans who entered its portals were few and far between. He had plenty of money on him, and there was invariably a hot "school" to be found there.

He had been playing for perhaps half an hour and winning steadily, when he asked the club proprietor to give Tessa's number a ring. The man later on remembered that it was at just on half-past twelve. He got an answer to the effect that Tessa was not home yet; a reply which had the result of rousing the brooding devil which was eating at Mascagni to fever pitch.

Where the hell was she? Who was she out with?

"*Dio mio*, Flo.!" one of the card-players grunted as for the third time Mascagni raked in a heavy pool. "Like-a dese Engleesa say: you lucky da cards, unlucky da love!"

Mascagni half-rose with a snarl, and in an instant would have been at the throat of the jester, but that he suddenly remembered that the fellow was a *Camorrista* man, and the come-back from a quarrel with him might be extremely unpleasant. With a muttered oath, he went on playing.

But, strangely enough, from that moment Mascagni's luck turned. He began to lose even more heavily than he had been winning before.

It was at about one o'clock that the phone rang, and Olinto Delmorti, the proprietor of the club, went to the instrument. It was Tessa Domenico, ringing Flo. Mascagni.

What transpired at the telephone must have been something which pleased the gangster, for, for the first time that night, the brooding scowl left his face and something like a smile took its place. When he came back to the card-table he was whistling.

"Not so unlucky in love, Giacomo," he observed to the elder man who had spoken. "I got a date in an hour so you'll know that I'm quitting then."

"*Si!*" the other answered. "But you lose-a da cards, now, Floriello. When I spoke, you win ever't'ing."

But, by a strange coincidence, Mascagni's luck changed again. In the next three-quarters of an hour all, and more, of the bundle of notes he had passed over had returned to him, and he got up a good winner. With a careless nod and the remark that they would finish it out another time, he left the club and turned up towards Oxford Street.

In a sort of subconscious way he noticed a little figure in a doorway opposite the *Circolo;* someone who, as far as height went, might have been a lad of twelve. As Mascagni moved on up the street, so also did he, but the gangster took no further notice of him.

Suddenly rain began to fall in a light drizzle, and Mascagni turned towards a back alley which he knew would give him a short cut towards that part of Oxford Street for which he was heading. He noticed, almost without realizing, that the small figure which had kept pace with him along the other side of the street had disappeared; then he heard him scuttling along the alley well in front of him. One of those pests of homeless kids who are to be found dossing in every second doorway in Soho, he supposed.

Along the alley he went, keeping under the lee side of the wall. Something, a shadow, suddenly moved in the recessed doorway of a warehouse right opposite him. He supposed it was that kid who had dodged in there out of the rain. Then, suddenly, and without the slightest sound or warning, the beam of a powerful torch shot straight into his face from that doorway opposite, momentarily blinding him. He flung his hand up to cover his eyes—and that was the last action of Floriello Mascagni on earth.

With incredible speed and force a knife flew across the dividing space, piercing his throat and pinning his head to the solid door behind him. Like a flash it was followed by the thrower, who plunged a second weapon right to his heart. With a groan, which was the last sound he ever made, he hung there limply for a second or two, then his weight dragged the first knife from the door and he collapsed in a heap immediately beneath it.

With that same swiftness with which he seemed to do everything, the little figure pulled the knife from his victim's throat and recovered the other. As calmly as though he were eating his dinner, he wiped both weapons upon the dead man's clothes and put them back in their sheaths. Systematically, he went through every pocket of Mascagni's clothes and emptied them, then slid out of the alley as noiselessly as he had entered it!

◇◇◇

Curiously enough it was that never-to-be-sufficiently-cursed nuisance, Paolo Vanadi, who found the body of the gangster. The mere fact of his being at large proved Fasoli's positive conviction that his belligerent customer had fallen into the hands of the police, as usual, to be entirely wrong.

One would have thought that, with his police record for bellicosity when in drink, the reveller from the North Country would have made a rush to find the nearest constable to prove that he had no complicity in the crime. Another strange fact, strange considering the condition he had been in but a little over two hours before, Signor Vanadi was now as sober as the proverbial judge and, instead of following what would seem to be the natural course for him to have taken, began to behave in an exceedingly strange manner.

First, in the light of a small torch he concealed beneath his coat, he examined the two dreadful wounds, then himself went through every pocket of the dead man's clothes, finding, of course, nothing. Then, in the same methodical way, he gave his attention to the door behind the dead man, found that cleft where the first knife had pinned Mascagni to the woodwork, and stood for a few moments in thought.

Giving his attention now to the doorway opposite and the cobbles between, he examined them carefully and apparently came to some decision concerning them. Following the alley along in the direction in which Mascagni had been moving, he found a tiny footprint marked clearly in blood, which showed him that someone, ostensibly a woman, though the foot, although short, was extraordinarily broad for its length, had not only been upon the scene, but must have been extremely close to the body to have stepped in the pool of blood in which it lay.

Still fainter traces of the same foot-spoor showed him that it had proceeded as far as Greek Street and then turned north. An examination of the other end of the alley showed him more than one trace of the way Mascagni had come. Apparently he had seen sufficient to stamp upon his mind some theory as to how the crime had been committed.

But something was still puzzling the signor; there was some little thing which, to judge by the frowning perplexity of his saturnine face, left an unanswered question in his mind—something which did not fit in. Returning to the body he again, and in the same cautious way, turned his torch upon it, and commenced a second search of Mascagni's clothing; it proved as futile as had the first. Suddenly he lifted one of the murdered man's hands, the right, and examined the finger-tips closely. Something he saw there brought from him a deeply-uttered, well-satisfied "Ah!"—it was a faint blue stain which marked the whorls of the dead man's first finger and thumb.

The puzzled expression had gone from the signor's face, and its place was taken by one of intense eagerness. Leaving the alley he made his way to the nearest telephone box and, in his weird, broken English, informed the police where they would find the murdered body of Floriello Mascagni. After which Signor Paolo Vanadi did something which would have considerably enlightened the denizens of Soho amongst whom he periodically paraded his wild antics.

Moving quietly to Dean Street, and first making very sure that there was no one hanging about in the immediate vicinity, he produced a latchkey and let himself into the lodgings of Detective Inspector McCarthy. Some half-hour later that officer emerged as his well-known self and, keeping well clear of the alley which by now he knew would be a hive of police, made his way by a circuitous route to the *Circolo Romagna*.

A very few minutes' earnest conversation with Olinto Delmorti—who had fear of the law in the very highest degree where Inspector McCarthy was concerned—sufficed to give the inspector the information he needed.

Firstly, that Mascagni had come into the *Circolo* somewhere in the region of a little after half-past eleven o'clock; that he had told Delmorti to put a call through to a certain number—carefully noted down by the inspector—and which was that of Tessa Domenico's lodgings in Doughty Street, off Holborn. That was at twelve-thirty; an hour later. He had learned that the beautiful Tessa had not returned home at that hour.

Secondly, that at one o'clock the phone rang and, answering it, Delmorti found it to be Tessa Domenico, asking for Mascagni. He was informed that the message must evidently have been an assignation made by Tessa for later that night, or, rather, that morning. Mascagni had been exceedingly cheerful about it and had informed his fellow-gamblers that he was finishing in something under the hour, as he had a date. He had left the club at about a quarter to two with quite a large number of notes in his possession.

"And," McCarthy thought to himself, "was found not six minutes' walk away, murdered, and with empty pockets!"

From the *Circolo*, McCarthy put through a police call to Exchange, and was promptly given the correct address of the number given to Delmorti as Tessa Domenico's. He quickly gleaned the further information that the subscriber was a Mrs. Flannigan and the house a boarding establishment. So much for that.

"Right," he said in parting, to the club proprietor. "You can keep the fact to yourself that I've been asking a few questions, Delmorti."

It was as he was leaving the place, followed by the well-nigh grovelling Delmorti, that he observed one man, a dark, swarthy-skinned Italian in the dress-clothes of a waiter, covered by an overcoat, who was seated alone. What quickly fastened the inspector's attention upon him was that his keen eyes detected more than one spot of blood upon the man's collar, and also upon his shirt-front. The latter marks had been made still more prominent by a vigorous attempt to rub them out!

Any person carrying bloodstains so close to the vicinity in which Mascagni was lying murdered was of considerable interest; moreover, the man's face showed signs of having been heartily battered, and not so long since. He had a lump between his neck and jaw which suggested that he might have been kicked by a horse!

"Who's that chap?" he asked, though without appearing to give the man any particular attention.

Carefully turning his back so that the man in question should have no suspicion that he was speaking about him, Delmorti informed McCarthy that the man's name was Andrea Praga, a waiter.

"He is not long com' to Soho," he informed McCarthy, confidentially. "He is no good—what you call a messee job, *Inspectore*. To-night 'e is sack forwit' from the *Hotel Splendide*, becos' he juggle wit' the change of a customer—*sapeti?*"

"That sort, is he?" McCarthy said. "But that doesn't explain where he got the pasting from."

"To-night," Delmorti informed him, in a still lower tone, "he run across a man called Paolo Vanadi—you know him, p'raps? One tough guy, so to spik. He com' here from the North each six months or so, and drinks all the wine in Soho."

"I fancy I have heard of him," McCarthy said, without move of a muscle.

"Well, to-night," the signor went on, "Vanadi he is ver' drunk in de street, and this Praga 'e tries to run da rule over 'im, for his mon'. Plenty mon' this Vanadi always has on him when 'e com' to Soho."

"He's luckier than I am, Delmorti," the inspector said. "Well?"

The signor shrugged his shoulders.

"Well, that ees what 'appened to 'im. P'raps it teach 'im to keep 'is 'ands in 'is own pockets."

McCarthy nodded. "We'll hope so," he said, as he turned towards the door. "I must have an eye kept on this Vanadi. We've got trouble enough in Soho without his sort bargin' in. Don't forget to forget that I've been in here making inquiries to-night," he cautioned. "So long."

Chapter XVII

"Big Bill" Does a Spot of Sleuthing

The inspector was in an exceedingly thoughtful mood as he made his way back to his Dean Street lodgings. The discovery of that tell-tale stain upon Mascagni's fingers had opened up a quite unexpected angle in the Soho Square crime. That Mascagni had been connected with it in some way or other had been patent from the fact that he had been in the car which had attempted to run him, or Regan, down that morning. But that the gang-boss had actually had the stolen prints through his hands was the very last thing McCarthy had ever dreamed of. But there was no gainsaying that stain; that told its own story, and that it could possibly have been there through any other medium was unthinkable.

Mulling it over in his mind there seemed only one possible way in which that could have occurred. Mascagni's mob, probably including Floriello personally, had committed the Anselmi murder and purloined the coffee-stall. When, right after that scream, the body of the butchered Rohner had been tossed into it, the prints had been hurriedly passed to Mascagni, in case anything should go wrong with the killer's getaway. He would have certain explicit orders concerning them, of course. The probability was that he had returned them only that night—in all likelihood to the mysterious personage whom McCarthy, on the prowl, had picked up leaving Fasoli's, only to lose him in that car. He would have given a month's salary to have caught even one glimpse of the face of that individual.

On the other hand there was another possibility to be considered: that Mascagni had still had them in his possession when he was done to death after leaving the *Romagna*, but, looking at it in every light, the inspector did not think so. But now that that tell-tale stain had made it a certainty that the dead gang-boss had had the prints in his possession, that intriguing business of the knock upon the window by the table at which the Baroness Lena Eberhardt regularly had her *déjeuner*, took on a totally different perspective. Had his first idea of that rather extraordinary happening been right, and the knock been a definite signal, or message, to the baroness? Looked at in the light of Withers' report as to her later movements, and particularly her amazing disappearance somewhere in the vicinity of Fasoli's, it certainly looked so.

That thought brought another to his mind: what had become of Withers who had an assignment with him to be somewhere on the prowl in the vicinity of the *Circolo Venezia* at about eleven o'clock? Not one sign of him had the inspector seen during his peregrination of the Soho streets, though, he admitted freely, the taxi would have had to have pulled up right under his very nose for him to have been aware of its presence. Still, the black-out was something Withers would have been well hardened to by now, and he would certainly have found McCarthy had he been on the spot as arranged. That he had not been, intrigued the inspector considerably, for as a rule the big taxi-man was the soul of reliability.

Dismissing the thought of Withers' lapse as of little consequence since he had not needed him, his mind reverted again to Mascagni and the sudden and terrible death which had been dealt out to him. That he well deserved it there was no question of doubt, and particularly so if he had had any hand in the equally brutal slaying of poor old Joe Anselmi, not to mention the butchery in Soho Square; but that was not the point. Murder was murder in the eyes of the law; no matter how much the murdered deserved the fate dealt out to him.

And in that connection there was another thing which puzzled McCarthy considerably—that tiny footprint which, he had no doubt whatever, had been left behind either by the killer or someone connected with him, and present, when the crime was committed. That it was the spoor of a man was impossible, albeit it seemed, despite its size, of an extremely ungainly shape to be left by a woman's modern shoe. Automatically his mind turned upon the only two women he knew to have been connected with Mascagni within the last twenty-four hours: the Baroness Lena Eberhardt (and behind her name there must be set a very large note of interrogation), and Tessa Domenico. The foot of the former, he remembered perfectly; during that lunch-hour he had had more than one opportunity of noticing, not only the perfect shape of her feet and ankles, but also the highly expensive perfection of the shoes she was wearing. He was as certain as he could be of anything that they had not left that particular spoor.

For one thing the baroness, although perfectly formed, was a woman of rather over average height, and built in proportion; her feet, though leaving nothing whatever open to criticism, were definitely of a long and narrow mould, quite different to the extremely short and thickish print he had found in the alley. And there was another side of that which could not be overlooked: if the Austrian woman were connected with this espionage gang who killed so readily, it would certainly not have been left to her to carry out the murder of Flo. Mascagni.

Just what the feet of the perfectly formed Tessa Domenico were like he could not recall to memory, but she, too, although the perfection of female anatomy, was upon the tall and stately side, and generously built. Her feet, he was certain, were not of the tiny variety which would account for so short a spoor. But there was one thing connected with her which certainly gave him to think, and think hard: that was the fact that, after being away from home at the time that Delmorti had rung up at Mascagni's request, she, at one o'clock, should put a call through there and make what undoubtedly was an assignation to meet Mascagni at a still later hour—possibly at two o'clock, since he had not left the *Circolo* till a quarter to that hour. Knowing all the short cuts of Soho backwards, Mascagni would have been able to get to Doughty Street comfortably by two o'clock, even handicapped by the black-out.

And Tessa Domenico, born and bred in Soho and, like most of its youthful denizens, having run its streets night and day for years, knew it as well as did her lover. She would know exactly which short cuts he would take to bring him out at the nearest point to Doughty Street. She would also have a fairly good idea just about what time he would leave the *Romagna*; he could, quite possibly, have told her that in their talk over the phone.

There came back to him Withers' words to the effect that Tessa still ran around with Mascagni though more from fear than any love she might have for him; a cynical comment with which he had agreed. Had she, for any ulterior motive arising out of that situation, had anything to do with the "removal" of the jealous lover she went in terror of? Had that phone call been the medium by which Flo. Mascagni had been put "on the spot"?

But there, again, he found himself up against a theory to which he could not give credence. If those footprints were to be taken as of any value at all towards the elucidation of the crime, then Tessa Domenico must have either committed the murder herself or at any rate been present when it had been done; neither of which possibilities—if only from the very method by which the murder had been committed, would, in his opinion, hold water for a single moment. And in the latter case why was there no spoor left by the murderer?

But the fact remained that the call making the assignation with Mascagni had come from Tessa Domenico and within a few minutes of leaving to join her he had been ruthlessly killed. If, again, this espionage gang with which he was undoubtedly connected had had anything to do with his death, then there was a possible argument that she, too, must be in some way connected with them. He could see it was not possible for them to have known, other than by information from herself, that Mascagni was leaving the club at the time he did, to keep an appointment with her. However, whichever way it was, that call would have to be followed up and the beautiful Tessa put through an interrogation which would leave nothing concerning her movements that night in doubt.

With Inspector McCarthy, to make up his mind was usually to act instanter, but he realized that to make for the boarding-house in Doughty Street at that hour of the morning, and, without warrant, or any other authority, pull the girl out of bed for an inquisition would be absolutely useless and, more than likely, defeat his own ends. He decided to turn in and get an hour or two's sleep.

Six o'clock saw him out of bed again, and dressing; less than an hour after that saw him out upon the street and this time the debonair, perfectly-groomed Inspector McCarthy that the world knew, and, knowing, had taken to its bosom.

He was proceeding along New Oxford Street when a taxi-cab coming along at an entirely illegal pace drew up with a screech of brakes beside him. In the driver's seat, penitence stamped indelibly upon his huge face, was Mr. William Withers, evidently making his way from his Clerkenwell residence.

"Guv'nor," he exclaimed, before McCarthy could utter a word, "I know just what you're a-goin' t' say, an' I ain't got no answer for it. I done in your job last night; leastwise," he qualified, "I never done it in intentional—only on account o' losin' me temper. When I got back again I couldn't find you nowhere."

"No bones broken, Withers," McCarthy returned equably. "As it turned out I didn't want you. Where did you get to anyway?"

"Well, it's this way, sir, an' I ain't makin' no excuses for meself. I was just makin' for Soho Square to come in by Greek Street, when a bleeder wiv a big car come slashin' out into Oxford Street wiv no lights on, takes the corner on two wheels and all-but rams me proper. He gave my mudguards a dam' good rakin'—'ow 'e didn't take 'em off is more than I know. Take a mike at 'em, guv'nor, an' you'll see as 'ow I ain't tellin' no lies—th' dirty arsterbar!"

McCarthy pricked up his ears and took a glance at the mudguards; their condition upon one side amply corroborated Withers' story.

"What time would this be?" he asked quickly, the recollection of that other car which had shot out into Oxford Street without lights strong in his mind.

"Just about five and twenty past eleven, sir," "Big Bill" answered promptly. "I'm sure of that becos I knew I was arter your time, havin' took on a short restarong job."

"Did you get the number of the car?"

"No, sir. 'Is rear-plate was all daubed up wiv mud or sunninck. Couldn't 'ave been mud though," he added reflectively, "becos we 'adn't 'ad no rain till a bit later."

"If it was the car I have in mind, Withers, it was done purposely," McCarthy said. "The front one would have probably been the same. It would be easy enough to get away with that in the black-out. Well, what happened?"

"Well, that's where I lost me temper, sir, an' done in your job. I shouts to th' bleeder, an' he don't take no more notice of me than if I was a bundle of muck. So rahnd I comes into Soho Square, and out again by way of Sutton Street and the Charin' Cross Road, and arter 'im. By that time he's got 'is rear light on, so's I can 'ang on to 'im."

"He kept on east?" McCarthy questioned.

"No, sir, that was only a fake. 'E runs along as far as Bloomsbury Street, turns in there to Bedford Square, and cuts through there back into Tottenham Court Road, and then back into Oxford Street agen, running west-bound."

"In other words he was doubling back on his track?"

"That's it, sir. 'E goes straight along to Park Lane then cuts into Upper Brook Street."

"Upper Brook Street!" McCarthy exclaimed. "That leads into Grosvenor Square, Withers."

"An' that's just where he did go to, sir, and wot's more 'e pulls up at that very 'ouse where that lady as I tailed to-day 'angs out."

A whistle came involuntarily from McCarthy's lips. Here, indeed, was something tangible at last.

"What did you do then, Withers?" he asked quickly.

"Nothink, sir. As soon as I see where 'e'd gorn to I pulls up sharp and took a chanst and doused my glims. Not that there's much of 'em to douse these 'ere black-out nights," he growled. "But I 'ops out o' the keb quick and starts fuddlin' rahnd wiv my ingin in case a cop comes so I'd 'ave some sort of a spiel that it 'ad failed. I reckoned as it was goin' to be more use to you, my 'anging on to this blighter as long as I could, than goin' up to the door and 'avin' a barge with 'im abaht my mudguards."

"Good work, Withers—great work," McCarthy applauded unstintingly. "And after that?"

"'E was in the 'ouse abaht half an hour, sir, an' when 'e comes aht, that there skirt as I followed from Verrey's come to the door with 'im, a-jawin' away sixteen to the dozen as the sayin' goes."

"Did you hear anything of what they were saying, Withers?" the inspector asked eagerly.

Withers shook his head. "No, sir. They was talkin' in some furrin langwidge—German, I think. The only thing as I 'eard was when he was at the gate he calls out, 'You'll see that Heinrich will be all ready to cross with the stuff to-morrow evening', an' she sez, '*Ja*', and something that sounded like 'Orf Weedershins.'"

"Auf Wiedersehen," McCarthy corrected. "And then…"

"And then 'e gits into the car agin an' turns an' goes back into Park Lane, and drives into the forecourt of that there noo block of flats as they've just opened up. 'E 'urries in there, and arter a minit or two a bloke comes out, a servant of some sort, and drives 'is car rahnd into the mews, and puts it away. I'm layin' nice and quiet over against the 'Ide Park railin's a-watchin'. I might a took a chanst and put in a question or two, but I thought as it might get back to 'Is Nibs, and mebbe do more 'arm than good. So I started back to Soho in the 'opes of findin' y'. When I couldn't, I beat it for 'ome and give you a ring up on the blower, but I couldn't get no answer. I'm sorry if I've mucked anythink up, guv'nor, by not bein' on time, but I done what I thought was the best thing."

"My dear Withers," McCarthy assured him, "a dozen of Scotland Yard's best men couldn't have done more. I'll see that something quite solid comes your way for last night's work."

Here, indeed, he was thinking, had the utterly unexpected come to pass through the agency of "Big Bill" Withers' native Cockney sagacity—plus a bit of sheer blind luck. He admitted the latter part of it freely, but all the luck in the world would not have availed much had it not been that Withers had used the old brain-box to the very fullest degree. Here, then, was a direct connection, an absolute linking up between Fasoli's dive and the aristocratic Baroness Lena Eberhardt.

When Withers had lost her in that unsavoury vicinity to-day it must have been to the *Circolo Venezia* that she had made her way. The same disreputable hole which Mascagni had left a little after eleven o'clock to go to the *Romagna*, from which he had been called to a terrible death by a phone message from Tessa Domenico. The quick ears of the obstreperous Paolo Vanadi had caught enough to tell him that Flo. Mascagni had an appointment with someone at Fasoli's for eleven o'clock, and at not much later than that hour the shadow he had followed had left that place—to make his way direct to the Baroness Lena Eberhardt's mansion in Grosvenor Square. With what—if not the prints which he must have recovered either from Mascagni, who at some time or other most certainly had handled them, or someone else in that place?

"You never got a chance to see the man's face, I suppose, Withers?" he asked. "Either in Grosvenor Square or outside those flats."

Withers shook his head negatively. "No, guv'nor, I never 'ad a chance at neither place. There was next to no light in the 'all in Grosvenor Square, and the outside of them there flats was as black as the 'obs of 'ell. And atop o' that, the bloke had 'is overcoat collar turned up to 'is ears, and 'is cady pulled dahn till you couldn't see nothink of his phisog fr'm any angle."

"It's a pity, Withers, but the connection is quite clear enough to make me certain of the man's identity—that is to say that it's the same person who I believe to be connected with the murder in Soho Square. And, also," he added, "with the killing of Floriello Mascagni early this morning."

"Mascagni!" Withers echoed. "Lumme they ain't bumped that rat off, 'ave they?"

"He'll never be deader, that's a certainty," McCarthy said. "And now you shall drive me as far as Doughty Street, and I'll have a few words with the lady who telephoned him to meet her less than an hour before he was found stabbed to death in an alley. Things are beginning to move, William; things are definitely beginning to move."

Chapter XVIII

Tessa Domenico Moves Upwards

When opposite the number of Tessa Domenico's boarding-house, the inspector instructed Withers to drive on a little way and pull up upon the opposite side of the road.

"I want to take a good look-see at the place before I make an entrance there. It's a queer thing, Withers, how the exterior of a place can tell you a divil of a lot about it and how it's run, but it certainly can."

He found it to be one of the large, double-fronted old Georgian houses of which a few are still left in the vicinity, though the greater majority of them have long since been transposed into offices, occupied for the greater part by solicitors. Outside the french windows of the first floor, and which appeared to all belong to one huge room, was one of the ornamental iron-railed balconies so beloved of our great-grandfathers.

Two of these were open, though not over-clean lace curtains prevented him from getting a glimpse into the room. One thing not to be missed was a large printed card hung in one of them which bore the legend "Large, Comfortable,

Front Bed-sitting-room To Let." There, he thought instantly, was his opening to get into the place and have a few quiet words with the landlady before questioning Miss Domenico herself. It was truly amazing how easily garrulous landl-adies could be pumped, and he wanted to verify the fact that that one o'clock call had been put through from the phone belonging to the house, and also that it had been sent by Tessa, herself. Past experience had made him well aware that very little went on in a boarding-house of that type without the landlady being cognisant of it, whether complacent or not.

He was just about to cross the road when a large and exceedingly expensive-looking car of Italian make drove up and stopped outside the door. From it, to his profound astonishment, there alighted the last one in the world he expected to see—the man with the icy eyes. Promptly McCarthy continued his leisurely stroll along the pavement, taking the precaution to jerk the brim of his own felt hat well down over his eyes; the last thing he wanted was for this man to glance across and recognize him. Fortunately, his quarry kept straight on, mounted the six or seven steps to the front door, and knocked. But before that had hap-pened a lady came quickly from the room opening on to the balcony and waved down to the caller, for whom she had evidently been waiting as she was wearing a hat and was obviously dressed for the street.

In answer to the knock the door opened and first a some-what slatternly-looking woman appeared at it to whom the man spoke, then turned back again and stood waiting by the door of the car. McCarthy noticed that it was driven by a uniformed chauffeur who was definitely peculiar in appearance. He was equally so in his behaviour, for he made no attempt to move and perform any of the usual offices common to men in his particular line of servitude.

He seemed to be perched up in some strange way that the inspector could not quite make out; indeed, was bolstered up like a sort of jack-in-the-box on cushions.

Nor did he attempt to get out and lend a hand when a domestic—as untidy-looking, by the way, as was her mistress—and a man who wore a sleeved waistcoat of a "boots," appeared and came down the steps bearing a brand-new and extremely expensive-looking trunk. This they proceeded to place upon the baggage rack at the rear of the car, which they left unfastened and hurried back, presumably to fetch another. Considerably to McCarthy's astonishment, the strange-looking chauffeur still sat rigidly behind his wheel and let them get on with it. When they reappeared with a second trunk of the same size and class, he did not as much as turn his head; evidently an extremely high and mighty person, this.

With the advent of the second trunk the "boots" proceeded to strap the two securely, for which he received an extremely handsome tip from the icy-eyed man, if one might judge by the pleasantly surprised look which came to his somewhat careworn face. McCarthy, eyeing the trunks and having a fairly decent idea of the cost of that quality of goods, found himself thinking that things were evidently on the boom with the fair (or, rather, extremely dark) Tessa.

Then that lady herself came through the door, clad now in a long chinchilla coat which McCarthy would have bet any money had never been purchased under four figures. He had too much experience in the recovery of stolen goods of that class not to be well aware of the prices at which they had been valued. Unquestionably old man Domenico's little girl had struck heights undreamed of by her hard-working father and mother. She was ushered into the equipage as though she were a queen, the icy-eyed man took his seat beside her, and it started off, running in the direction of Holborn.

Instantly that special sense which gives the born sleuth of men an inkling of the motives of those in whom he is interested, began to work furiously in McCarthy's mind. Why was Tessa Domenico breaking ground within a few hours of the cold-blooded murder of the man she had given an appointment to so short a while since, and whom it was understood that she was very shortly to marry? If one could judge by the calm serenity of her Madonna-like countenance she was either one of two things: either utterly callous where Mascagni's death was concerned, or else in complete ignorance of it. And what was at the bottom of the man with the icy eyes coming for her, like some sort of modern Prince Charming after Cinderella, and in a car which certainly cost considerably more than any glass coach which had ever been built?

Those brand-new, luxury-built trunks? How were they to be accounted for in the light of the fact that no later than one o'clock that morning Tessa had phoned her man—as all Soho and Saffron Hill knew him to be—and called him to her side? Now here was Mascagni murdered, and Tessa off with a man of very different status. The two things did not fit; there was a nigger in the wood-pile somewhere, as far as the beautiful Tessa was concerned.

"After them, Withers," he instructed, upon hurrying back to the cab, "and for the Lord's sake play canny. I don't want to arouse the slightest suspicion in the minds of that pair that they are being followed."

From Holborn the trail held straight on into Oxford Street, and from there to the corner of Park Lane, into which it turned and swung into the forecourt of the newly-erected set of mansion flats to which Withers had trailed the man earlier that morning, and which were certainly as expensive to rent as anything to be found in the West End of London.

Their prices, McCarthy happened to know, were enough to make even the ultra-rich blink.

The car drew up outside the main entrance and a huge, imposingly-attired linkman, whose face the inspector recognized instantly as one known to him somewhere or other, and professionally, came out and opened the door of the car for them. Then, as they passed through into the ornate communal hall of the building, the linkman invoked two further uniformed attendants by a shrill of the whistle he carried.

"Blimey, guv'nor," "Big Bill" exclaimed through the small wicket window. "Take a mike at that big stiff, Jim Delaney, all dossed up like a flamin' major-general! I'll swear as 'e wasn't on duty last night when this bloke drove in. But it's the same car right enough; you can see the marks on 'is mudguard where he scraped mine."

McCarthy emitted a low whistle. "That's right, Withers," he said, "I've been trying to think where I'd known that fellow before. Delaney—I wonder how he picked up this particular job? Another case of forged references, I expect."

Which suspicion was a perfectly reasonable one as the gentleman had, and not so very long since, been suspected of having been concerned in one or two West End flat burglaries upon premises of which he had been the caretaker. Although he had got clear of the charge in each case only by the skin of his teeth, the police had something considerably stronger than suspicion that the imposing-looking caretaker had actually been the "inside" accomplice in the job.

Prior to this Mr. Delaney had a police-record which included several quite solid "stretches," and how he had ever got this particular post, except by means of "cooked" references, was decidedly beyond McCarthy. He must have had a "pull" somewhere; it might even have been that someone connected with the premises knew his story and that he had decided to run straight in the future. More power to his elbow if he had. But…it was with a very dubious shake of his head that the inspector dismissed Mr. Delaney from his mind for the moment—but only for the moment.

Meantime, from their vantage over against the park railings, they watched the two attendants unstrap the trunks and prepare to lift them down. Upon this occasion, however, the chauffeur decided to superintend matters and got down. To the inspector's astonishment the man, for all his entirely deceptive width of shoulder and height when seated upon his cushioned perch, was a veritable dwarf, scarcely more than four feet high. As he walked around the car, first stopping a moment to examine, frowningly, the marks upon the two mudguards, he looked as much like a large chimpanzee dressed up in a uniform as anything else.

"Blimey!" ejaculated the gentleman whose car had caused those marks, "there's a flaming runt for y'! Damme, 'e's no 'igher than a bantam! That's right, cock," he adjured the dwarf, "git an eyeful; you won't look them dents and scratches off in an 'urry."

"How the divil does he ever work his clutch and foot-brake with those short legs, Withers?" McCarthy asked perplexedly.

"Don't arst me, sir. 'E must 'ave some sort o' gadgets rigged up; 'e'd never git at 'em with them stumpy legs of 'is, that's a cert."

"Must be something of that sort," McCarthy agreed. The thought crossed his mind that the dwarf must be an extremely valued personal servant in more ways than one, for no man in his sane senses, without individual knowledge of the person in question, would have ever chosen such a peculiarly built individual to drive a car of that size and quality.

While the thought was in his mind the dwarf hopped back on to his perched-up seat, and the car began to move slowly away from the door.

"It's a hundred to one that he's taking it into its garage," McCarthy said quickly. "After it. Make sure of where it's parked and get back here as soon as you can. I'm going to have a word with our friend Delaney."

To say that the ex-suspect was startled at the sudden and totally unexpected appearance of Detective Inspector McCarthy was to considerably understate the emotion visible in the man's countenance. From a ruddy, entirely healthy colour, his face turned a mixture of grey and a delicate cucumber-green.

"Ah, Delaney!" McCarthy hailed in that soft, emollient voice of his. "Here we are again, y' see!"

The man cast a fearful glance into the hall where the two porters could be heard handling the luggage into an elevator.

"I—I've done nothing, Inspector!" he commenced, when McCarthy cut him off with an airy wave of his hand.

"No one has said ye did, James," he said quietly. "All that I'm asking for is a little information—official information," he added significantly. "And the more of it I get from you, of the right kind, the more forgetful I'm likely to be of—of other things."

In less than two minutes McCarthy had acquired the information that the lady and gentleman who had just arrived were the Count and Countess Hellner—Austrian nobility he understood! That the gentleman had taken the most expensive furnished suite in the mansion for himself and his spouse some three days ago; that his luggage had not as yet arrived.

That the rent of that particular flat—he pointed it out as the one showing six balconied windows on the right hand of the front and overlooking Park Lane and that *plaisance* itself—was fifteen hundred pounds a year, and that, taking it all round, the mere acquisition of such a flat was a guarantee not only of extreme financial solvency, but also of respectability, as the inquiries made by the manager in both directions were exhaustive.

There were quite a number of other things which McCarthy either wheedled or forced from the big linkman which more than ever strengthened the opinion that, where the beautiful Tessa Domenico was concerned, there was very definitely something more afoot than met the eye.

One last, but most pregnant question he put to the linkman.

"And I suppose, James," he said, "that if I wanted to pay a little visit to the flat, purely an official visit, ye'll understand, without the formality of being taken up and announced, or, for the matter of that, anyone knowing about it, it could be managed?"

A rather scared look came into the man's face.

"Don't forget it's Scotland Yard that's asking, Delaney," he said quietly. "And we don't forget little favours."

"I—I suppose…" Mr. Delaney got out nervously.

"Then that's all right," McCarthy cut him off cheerfully. "I may look along later—perhaps at a time when ye could make it convenient to be at some duty that takes ye from the front door. Not that that'll matter!"

At that moment Withers' cab returned and parked in the place in which it had stood before.

"I'll be seeing you, James—I'll be seeing you," McCarthy murmured pleasantly.

With another wave of his hand he departed and took his seat in the taxi.

"I think," he said, "we'll take a quick run back to Doughty Street first. I fancy a word with Tessa Domenico's landlady is indicated. I beg her pardon—the Countess Something Hellner."

McCarthy's one question to that lady was brief and to the point. Did her late lodger, Miss Tessa Domenico, send out a call from the telephone belonging to the house at one o'clock that morning? The landlady's answer was quite as terse and equally to the point. Miss Domenico had not, and for the very simple reason that since leaving the house at about half-past eleven the night before, she had not returned to it until half-past seven this morning.

"Sich goings on," she was commencing with a virtuous snort, when McCarthy cut her short.

"I know; I know," he interrupted with a glance over the dingy hall. "Sich goings on have never been known in your respectable household before. Well, I believe y', madam, but there are thousands that wouldn't—including the lads of the 'E' Division, Metropolitan Police."

But, in spite of this jocosity McCarthy left the place in thoughtful, indeed, in an extremely grim mood.

Chapter XIX

McCarthy Paralyses His Superior Officer

It was somewhere in the region of midday that Sir William Haynes' phone rang out sharply; lifting the receiver he found that the man who happened to be uppermost in his thoughts at the moment was on the line to him—Detective Inspector McCarthy.

"I say, Mac," he exclaimed. "They seem to have been going it very hot in Soho last night. Do you know that there's been a third murder there since midnight?"

"Indeed? Who is it this time?" McCarthy asked in a voice which suggested that the subject was a matter of complete indifference to him.

"You'll never guess in a hundred years," the A.C. returned, almost excitedly.

"I'm not trying," the inspector said calmly. "If it's Flori-ello Mascagni you mean, I could have told you that within a quarter of an hour of the time of the murder. And let me correct you upon another point, Bill. Old Joe Anselmi, who I take it is one of the three you mention, was murdered before midnight, *not* after. Not so very long before, possibly only ten minutes or so, but the first duty of an Assistant Commissioner of Police is to have his facts right."

"You knew about Mascagni then?" the A.C. asked, somewhat snappily for him.

"Between you and I, Bill—or p'raps it's you and me, blest if I know—I was the first that knew anything about that particular bump-off; to be precise, I discovered the body and notified the police—when I'd done with it."

"You discovered…"

"I discovered the body and notified the police," McCarthy repeated. "And it wasn't any too pretty a sight. Nothing to be compared with the 'lady' of Soho Square, of course, but you don't see that kind of butchery every day—the Lord be thanked."

"Anything new in that direction, Mac?" Sir William asked avidly.

"Quite a number of things," McCarthy answered placidly, "though they are not ready to be the subject of a full official report yet awhile. When they are I fancy they'll make nice juicy reading for the Sunday newspapers."

"Where are you ringing from now?" the A.C. wanted to know.

"From a telephone-booth not far from Oxford Street," McCarthy informed him. "I've been doing quite a little bit of running round this morning, Bill—long before you were out of your bed, I daresay. By the way, old sawbones turned up with most unusual alacrity at the mortuary after you'd rung him up. You must have used the honeyed tongue on him, Bill; he was as bucked as the divil."

"Did he get anything useful out of his P.M., that's the big thing. Anything that is going to help us stop those plans getting out of the country, Mac?" he asked anxiously.

"We'll do that, all right," McCarthy assured him. "I want you to lend a hand and without asking any questions, Bill.

There's a certain dirty hole of a wine shop called the *Circolo Venezia* that I want watched. And when I say watched I don't mean that I want eight tons of human beef spread out all round it so that no one could mistake either who they are, or what they're at. I want clever youngsters put on to this game; chaps who don't look police, or act like them—that clear?"

"Perfectly. You won't give me any inkling of what's afoot?"

"I'll tell you this much, Bill. Those plans passed through that joint of Fasoli's last night, and in my opinion one man who had something to do with them was Floriello Mascagni. Whether it was through them that he was murdered, I can't say; but I'm quite certain of one thing, and that was that he was put 'on the spot,' definitely. There's another angle of that crime looming up very strongly, and it looks very much to me as though a hunch, a quite unexplainable hunch I had is going to turn up trumps. However, you see to the Fasoli side of it, and if any of the big bugs of the H.O. or the War Office start worryin' your little guts about those plans tell them that you've reason for believing that they'll be back in official hands before the day is out."

"That will put me in a most invidious position if they're not, Mac," Haynes said worriedly.

"Forget it," McCarthy responded lightly, "let your mind dwell upon the glory that'll be yours when you do hand 'em back."

Without warning he made one of those sudden and disconcerting switches of his.

"By the way, Bill, have you been to the Baroness Lena Eberhardt's house lately? I should perhaps say how long is it since you paid her a visit?"

"What has that to do with it?" Sir William asked sharply.

"The business of the interrogated is to answer questions as simply and directly as possible, not ask others in return which are merely evasive replies," McCarthy said whimsically.

"You shoot from one thing to another like a—a…"

"Gadfly," McCarthy supplied. "I repeat the question, Bill, how long since you visited at the Baroness Lena Eberhardt's house?"

"Although I still don't see what that has to do with the business in hand, I'll answer you. I should think it's a matter of quite a couple of months since I had a cup of afternoon tea there."

"Look at that, now!" McCarthy said softly. "The A.C. takes afternoon tea with the beautiful baroness in her mansion in Grosvenor Square. And I suppose," he continued, "that during that, or any other previous calls you might have made, the possibilities are that you might have met some of her friends."

"Of course I've met some of her friends—any amount of them. The baroness is one of the best known and most popular women in society—you'd have a hard job to go anywhere without meeting acquaintances of hers."

"Ah, evasive again, Bill," the inspector chided. "I wasn't speaking about her social acquaintances. I meant her own intimate friends, those to be met at her house."

"I have met some who might be called her really intimate friends," the Assistant Commissioner replied, the note of perplexity strong in his voice. "And I've met them at her house."

"Ah!" came softly from McCarthy. "Now we're getting somewhere. And were any of them Austrian, like herself, Bill? I mean those who were lucky enough to light out prior to Hitler's precious *anschluss*, or even after?"

There was a moment's pause before Sir William answered.

"Some of them were, Mac. Look here, what's at the bottom of all this questioning?"

"Just give me the answers, Bill, and leave what's at the bottom of it to me," the inspector returned smoothly. "Believe me I'm not wasting the breath I'll be wanting one of these fine days. You're quite sure," he proceeded, "that they *were* Austrian, and not German, by any chance? I reckon to know my Continentals fairly well, but there are times when I've a devil of a job to tell the difference."

The troubled note came into the A.C.'s voice again.

"So far as I can tell you, Mac, they were Austrians, but I may have been mistaken, of course. They certainly were introduced to me as Austrians, mostly of the class we're speaking of. I've no reason for doubting the baroness. Have you?" he shot swiftly.

"Me? The good Lord forbid that I should take any such liberty! What about her servants? Did any of them that you might have run across strike you as being of the true Teuton breed?"

Again there was a pause before Haynes answered.

"N-no," he answered, on a long-drawn thoughtful note. "I can't say that any I've encountered did."

"What about Heinrich?" McCarthy questioned. "Do you know which of 'em he happens to be?"

"Heinrich; Heinrich," Haynes repeated. "Yes, I do happen to know that particular one. He's her butler—a confidential servant who she brought with her from Vienna."

"Look at that, now," McCarthy said again, in that soft, enigmatic way he had. "And is there anything about Heinrich which might lead you to think that *he* was of Teutonic origin?"

"Well," Haynes answered thoughtfully. "Come to that, Mac, as far as build and general appearance goes he certainly *could* be German—of the old under-officer type that we got so familiar with in the war. But, of course," he added hastily, "that doesn't say that he is German for a moment. I can't believe that a lady who hates the Nazis and all their works as much as she does would have a German for her *major-domo*, for that I understood was practically the man's position there."

"It doesn't seem very likely—does it," McCarthy said emolliently, in fact so much so, that it added considerably to the perplexity of mind of his superior officer.

"Look here, Mac," he snapped. "Let's have done with all this. I hate to say it, but as your superior officer I demand to know what's at the bottom of all this questioning. You've something in your mind, and it's my business to know what it is. What is it that you're trying to say as far as the Baroness Lena Eberhardt is concerned?"

"Now, now, now," McCarthy chided. "Temper, Bill, does no good to anyone and, in particular, clouds the judgment of those who sit in high places—like yourself. The question really at the bottom of my mind is when are you likely to take tea with the lady again? Now don't fly off the handle; just give the question your kind consideration and the questioner a civil answer."

Across the line McCarthy heard the Assistant Commissioner choke down something. "I have an invitation to look in upon the baroness any time that I'm passing," he said stiffly, and with obvious effort.

"The invitation extended to you again no later than yesterday perhaps?" McCarthy questioned.

"If it's any part of your business, that is so," Haynes answered tartly.

"It's very much my business, Bill," the inspector told him. "And what's more you needn't go all up stage and high hat about it. If you'll do what I want you to, you'll drop in for that same cup of tea quite unannounced this afternoon, keeping in your mind the suggestion I've made concerning Heinrich, the lady's butler, *major-domo*, or whatever you like to call him."

That the Assistant Commissioner was paralysed with astonishment by the request was very palpable from the tone in which he answered it.

"You mean that?" he asked incredulously. "This isn't some…"

"This isn't anything but the proper prosecution of the job you've assigned me to," McCarthy said seriously. "I've my own reasons, and very good ones, for wanting someone who has an official eye to run the rule over that particular man, and any others he gets the opportunity of sizing up. There's no one else at the Yard who can do it, without arousing suspicion, and that at the moment is the last thing I want. It's up to you, of course. You're the lad with the say so, not me."

A certain note in the inspector's voice told the A.C. that, whatever there might be of what McCarthy called "phlahoolic" in his usual make-up, at the present moment he was absolutely serious.

"All right, Mac," he said, though reluctantly. "Since you think it's necessary, I'll go. Though what the woman will think of my turning up in that way, I'm dam'd if I know. I'll have to invent some excuse about being in the immediate neighbourhood, and try to make it sound plausible. But I can tell you this," he concluded grimly, "that if…"

"If everything doesn't turn out one hundred per cent good," McCarthy cut in, "the good Lord help Patrick Aloysius McCarthy, for nobody else at the Yard will. I'll chance it. You be there, Bill, and for the love of Mike," he went on incorrigibly, "don't forget any of the pretty little parlour tricks your mama taught you at her knee. Be a credit to the Force, and the Force will be a credit to you. And for all you know there may be other distinguished guests drop in to keep you company. You never can tell, as Mr. Bernard Shaw says."

And before the Assistant Commissioner could find any suitable retort to this persiflage, McCarthy had rung off, leaving Sir William Haynes using language totally unfitted for an ex-officer and gentleman, not to mention one of the high executives of New Scotland Yard.

Chapter XX

McCarthy Strikes a Snag

It was about three o'clock in the afternoon when Withers' cab pulled up again against the Hyde Park railings opposite that magnificent set of mansion flats. In his little box-office in the hall, ex-convict James Delaney was perusing the pages of an afternoon paper when a shadow fell across him which made him start. He started still more when he discovered the identity of the person who threw that shadow—Detective Inspector McCarthy!

"In?" the inspector questioned, with a jerk of his head upstairs.

"Out," Delaney answered somewhat nervously. "Not expected back till about four-thirty. First floor, and first door to the right. It's right next to the lift."

"I'll use the stairs," the inspector said. "Lifts are an idle habit."

Without another word he turned up a magnificent marble staircase. As he did so, out of the corner of his eye he saw Delaney hurriedly depart along the hallway.

The landing, off which a corridor little less in opulence than the hallway ran, was entirely empty. Not a sign of a living person was there to be seen, either at that level or on the stairs leading upwards. Taking a picklock from his pocket, he deftly inserted it in the keyhole of that door to the right of the elevator, gave a couple of cunning twists, then pushed it open and walked quietly in.

He found himself in an inner, small, but again ornately-furnished hall which led into a large drawing-room. Crossing to the front windows he saw that they looked directly down upon Park Lane. From the balcony outside he could have hailed Withers as easily as from the pavement.

He very quickly decided that this particular room would have no interest for him. It was too newly occupied to contain anything likely to be of use to him. But he looked about it and attended to one or two things which might prove serviceable later. From that he passed into a bedroom very nearly as large, and certainly quite as ornate as the drawing-room itself. Here had been placed those brand-new, expensive trunks which Tessa Domenico had removed from her lodging in Doughty Street that morning. They were still locked, and, apparently, had not been touched since the servitors of the flats had set them down. He would give them some personal attention as soon as he had been right through the flat; experience had told him that it was bad business not to know the lay of the land in any place where trouble might come upon you at any moment.

Out of this commodious sleeping apartment was a completely marbled bathroom which surpassed anything he had ever had the pleasure of taking his ablutions in, even in the most expensive hotels. It was double-doored; the one leading from the bedroom, and another opening into a dressing-room attached, which again opened on to an inner corridor which contained four doors.

Trying the first he came to, he discovered it to be that of another bedroom. Closing the door after him he went on to the next; it too was yet another, and even these palpably extra, or "spare," rooms were furnished in a state to make an ordinary man stare. No question that if these particular flats were, as they were accredited with being, the most expensive in London, they certainly gave the person who leased them something for their money.

He was about to pass on to the third of the doors when a sound reached his ear which sent him tense and listening intently for all that he was worth. Although two rooms and a corridor separated him from it he was quite certain that he had heard the snap of the outer door lock, if not that of the one which led into that magnificent drawing-room. Retracing his steps quickly to the dressing-room he listened there a moment; it was all he needed to assure him that the occupants of the flat had quite unexpectedly returned, and that he was caught in an anything but enviable position.

Slipping back again into the corridor he searched for a service door of any kind which might afford an exit, but there was none. The dining-room of the flat, from which there probably was a service door, was entered from the drawing-room and lay back from the front. To get at it he would have to pass through the bedroom and drawing-room, the chances of which, without being observed, were absolutely a million to one against. While he was endeavouring to make up his mind as to his best line of action, Tessa Domenico sailed through into the bedroom, followed by her male companion, and rendered those chances absolutely *nil*.

On tip-toe McCarthy crept to the bathroom door, opened it noiselessly the tiniest bit to see just how the land lay. More than ever were things unpropitious, for while Tessa had thrown off the magnificent chinchilla coat she had been wearing and tossed it upon the bed with her hat, and was evidently about to repair the ravages of her toilet, the man with the icy eyes simply leaned lazily against the door through which McCarthy must necessarily pass to get out. Which, in the inspector's opinion, put the tin hat on things entirely.

That neither had the faintest suspicion that there was any third party in the flat became evident from the turn their conversation took. The man was as calm and as placid as he had been when he had walked out of Signora Spadoglia's restaurant the night before, but the tone of Tessa Domenico's voice proved that she was at least agitated, if some much stronger emotion was not dominating her at the moment.

"Where did you hear that they were hard at work following up his"—her voice trembled for an instant—"his, Mascagni's death?" she asked.

He took a cigarette from his case and lit it before replying.

"Did you not expect that they would?" he returned with complete casualness. "My dear Tessa, such are the strange ways of this country of yours that the police give just as much attention to the murder of a gangster as they would to that of the Prime Minister. The outcry in the newspapers will of course be less, but otherwise the *modus operandi* will be exactly the same."

It struck instantly upon McCarthy, experienced as he was in the different gradations of the English tongue as spoken in cosmopolitan Soho, that this man was unquestionably German although speaking perfect, but pedantic, English. There was nothing colloquial in his phrasing. He reminded McCarthy both in his method of speech and his idiom more of that unconscious humorist, Lord Haw-Haw of Hamburg, than anyone he had ever heard. The only difference lay in a certain sinisterness which was behind this man's voice which the German broadcaster completely lacked.

"Speaking entirely personally," he went on, "I think there is little to fear from the outcome of Scotland Yard's activities. They do not strike me as having anything of either genius or inspiration behind them. For your reassurance I may say that Ludwig has performed the act of, shall we say, elimination too often to leave behind him any trace whatever for them to take hold of. 'Clue' is, I believe, the word I should have used."

McCarthy watching her as she sat before her mirror, saw a shudder of repulsion run through the beautiful Tessa.

"I hate that horrible dwarf!" she exclaimed. "I am afraid of him."

"Alliterative—and most unfair," he observed. "You have nothing whatever to fear from Ludwig. As a matter of fact he performed you a signal service in removing what threatened to be a very considerable danger from your path."

Had McCarthy been one of the animal species he would, to use that well-frayed term, have "pricked up his ears." So that dwarf chauffeur had been the actual killer of Floriello Mascagni—at the instigation of this cold-blooded German, of course. Had that freak also been the murderer of the Rohner individual? McCarthy doubted it, certain evidences plainly to be seen in the doorway in which the gangster had been murdered, showed that he had been first struck by a well-flung knife. In the Soho Square case the situation must have been entirely different: whoever had killed Rohner had certainly grappled with him, and held him by sheer strength while the ghastly deed was committed. To judge by the physique of the female impersonator that would have been entirely out of the question in the case of the dwarf despite the strength of trunk and arms he undoubtedly was possessed of. Again in the case of Harper, McCarthy was certain that the wound which had given the unusually tall, and powerful, constable his quietus had been delivered direct by hand—the dwarf could scarcely have reached the point below Harper's shoulder where the death wound had been inflicted. Unless he was entirely mistaken the man who had committed the dual murders in Soho Square was standing but a few feet from him at that moment.

"All the same," she said nervously, "I wish some other way had been found to get rid of Floriello."

Again he shrugged those athletic-looking shoulders of his and glanced at her amusedly.

"And what other way could possibly have been so efficacious?" he asked, and his tone suggested that the whole matter was one of the most complete indifference to him. "Do you think that a gangster and blackmailer such as he was could have been bought off—for any length of time? He had threatened your life repeatedly in the event of your having the audacity to look with favourable eyes upon any other but himself. You had no doubt whatever in your mind that he meant those threats, and would most assuredly carry them out."

"That is true enough," she admitted. "He would have killed me sooner or later."

He nodded his agreement. "Exactly; he had all the instincts of a wild beast, without the courage of one. Extermination was the only way to deal with him. He also had had the temerity to threaten me, though in a totally different connection. You, yourself, informed me that he was uttering threats against me no later than last night."

"I repeated to you just what he said; that he meant it, I have no doubt whatever."

"Nor I; he was that class of human rat. It so happens," he continued, "that I am not the man to brook threats of any sort or kind from anyone. I gave him the very fullest opportunity to translate his vicious words into action last night at Fasoli's. I humbled him into the dirt where he belonged, but there was nothing coming from him." He gave a short, hard laugh. "That sealed his fate as far as I was concerned. And now," he said, "let us have an end of it. He was useful for a time and, having outlived that usefulness, has met the only fate possible to the useless of this world."

He concluded with a gesture which McCarthy read as dismissing the subject of Floriello Mascagni once and for all, then with that slow step of his crossed the room and deposited the butt of his cigarette in a receptacle in the centre of the room. At the same moment the girl got up, lifted her hat from the bed and pulled it on again, eyeing herself in the mirror as she did so. The man, Hellner, Delaney had called him, lifted the chinchilla coat and held it for her. Evidently, McCarthy thought gleefully, the pair were off out again—the well-known Luck of the McCarthy's was doing its bit splendidly! In that noiseless way of his he backed out through the dressing-room and into that corridor in which were the four bedrooms, closing the doors cautiously behind him.

He did not move again until he heard for the second time that sharp sound of that outer door being closed after them, and even then it was only as far as the bathroom door to make sure that both had departed. For some minutes he stood listening intently, but not the slightest sound came to him. He might have chanced creeping as far as the drawing-room windows and taking a peep down but for the fact that the curtains of the ornate apartment were drawn, and a quick glance upwards on the part of either Hellner or the girl might upset his apple-cart completely. He determined first to continue his examination of those bedrooms; in one or other of them must be the man's luggage, since he had seen no sign whatever of it in the rooms he had already been through. Delaney had said something about it, but just what, had slipped his memory. He questioned much if Tessa's new belongings would hold anything to interest him.

One by one he completed his examination of the rooms, to find nothing of what he sought. Evidently Hellner's personal belongings had not yet arrived.

He was turning back into the corridor again when he caught sight of some inset panelling which might be quite easily the well-camouflaged entrance to a box-room. He was stooping to examine it when without the slightest warning that meticulously spoken voice he had been listening to but a little while before invited him to lift his hands, and quickly; at the same moment what was only too palpably the muzzle of a revolver or automatic pistol was jammed hard into the small of his back. The menace behind the quiet tone was all-sufficient to tell McCarthy that the quicker that request was obeyed the better.

But, almost involuntarily, McCarthy had swung round, to find the weapon speedily transferred to the pit of his stomach and himself staring into the utterly unmoving, though now narrowed ice-blue eyes. He now saw that that which had prodded him in the back was an automatic pistol, complete with its silencer, of a calibre to make short work of anyone it was discharged into. For just one split-second there flashed through the inspector's brain the thought that he would take a chance and attack, but the eyes so contemptuously regarding him were no longer blank and expressionless; there was that in their pale hardness which told McCarthy that this man would kill without the slightest compunction. The one hope he had was to play for a bit of time and seize upon whatever chance the other might give him—which was not likely to be much.

"Things," he remarked pleasantly, and with his unquenchable smile, "seem to have come slightly unstuck."

"Very much so, as far as you are concerned," the other retorted in an equally equable tone.

"Perhaps," McCarthy bluffed. "I think I have the pleasure of speaking to Mr.—or is it Baron?—Hellner?"

"That name will do as well as any other. To simplify matters we will agree upon Hellner—Baron Hellner. And you, I understand, are Detective Inspector McCarthy, of Scotland Yard."

"*New* Scotland Yard," McCarthy corrected in the same affable way. "Though it's a common error among foreigners."

The other gave him a cold smile—too chill and wintry to be propitious, the inspector thought.

"May I ask what you are doing here?" Hellner questioned.

"Now I should have thought that that would have been instantly apparent to a gentleman of your intelligence," McCarthy countered brightly. "Still if you want it in so many words I was endeavouring to search the place, under the mistaken idea that yourself and the Signorina Domenico had gone out again."

"We should have done so but for the blindest piece of chance," Hellner informed him, in that pedantic English of his. "Fortunately for me, and definitely unfortunately for you, in assisting the 'signorina,' as you call her, on with her coat, I chanced to glance into her mirror at a certain angle. That angle gave me a perfect view of yourself, concealed behind, and peeping out from the bathroom door. I could have shot you down there and then, McCarthy," he went on grimly, "and, under other circumstances would most assuredly have done so. But as the lady happens to be already in a highly nervous condition, I had no wish to startle her into some hysterical action which might not have suited my purpose. One has to think of these things."

Chapter XXI

The Tables are Turned

McCarthy nodded. "I see your point," he said gravely. "It's a thousand to one she'd have screamed like the divil and probably brought people on to the scene that ye'd not be wanting here—not at the moment. And after all," he proceeded as though arguing some point of interest quite detachedly, "it's only to be expected that a woman of that type *would* be in a high state of nerves when she knows that, not only is she connected with a wholesale murderer, but has been part and parcel, not to say an accessory before and after, the fact of one particular killing last night, which the police have already well in hand. Indeed, as the officer in charge of the case, I don't think there is a great deal of doubt that the gentle Tessa sent the telephone message that put Mascagni on the spot for that dirty little dwarf of yours to kill. Ludwig, d'ye call him?"

The pale eyes, watched so closely by McCarthy, seemed to become even fainter in colour if that were possible, and most certainly the look of menace in them deepened. But the man had evidently tight hold upon himself and never for one second did he betray anger or even exasperation.

"I think Inspector McCarthy can scarcely claim credit for information gained by listening-in to a private conversation?" he remarked.

"Not at all; not at all," the inspector hastened to agree. "But it was mighty helpful and is going to save a lot of time, and money. It'll be a matter of a very few hours before Herr Ludwig will find himself behind bars, on his way to the gallows *via* the Old Bailey."

"That is as maybe," Hellner said acidly. "To quote your English saying, a lot of water will run under the bridges between this and then."

"Don't you believe it, Herr Baron," McCarthy said heartily. "We don't make many mistakes about murderers in this country, once we know that they are. And social status makes no difference. We'll hang you just as quickly for the murder of the spy who called himself 'Madame Rohner,' and also for the wicked killing of Constable Harper at the back gate, as we will that misshapen chauffeur of yours."

"Is that so?" the German asked quietly, and McCarthy glancing down noticed that his finger tensed upon the trigger.

"That *is* so," he answered promptly. "Now that is a little bit of work I rather pride myself on," he continued, "particularly when you consider the time I've had on the job. My first impression that you were the murderer was what I'd call a pure 'hunch.' That's an American word, by the way; I don't know whether you've anything in German to exactly correspond with it. It merely means a sort of instinct. It was owing to that 'hunch' that I followed you out of Soho Square, and later set a certain friend of mine to follow you up. And it was there, Herr Baron, that you made your first big mistake—if you don't mind my pointing it out."

"Certainly not. One lives and learns."

"I somehow have the feeling that you'll not be doing either for long," McCarthy informed him, with a shake of his head. "Your first mistake was in not leaving Danny Regan just where your friends—men of Flo. Mascagni's gang, by the way—laid him out. It wouldn't have altered things actually, but it would have taken a little more time before I, personally, could have connected up the woman found dead on Hampstead Heath with the person killed in Soho Square. And equally," he went on significantly, "before I connected the *pseudo* Madame Rohner with the person who had stolen plans of certain anti-aircraft dispositions from Whitehall that afternoon."

That that was a totally unexpected shaft, and one which struck home, was very palpable to the inspector. For just an instant the pale eyes seemed to glaze and again that trigger finger tautened. But the man kept complete command of his voice when he put his next question.

"And how did that miracle of efficiency come to pass?"

"Perfume," McCarthy answered laconically. "A certain odour was unmistakable in the room at Whitehall from which the plans were stolen. It hung heavily upon the air at the scene of the Rohner killing—where, by the way, you left a stiletto and a lace handkerchief behind you. That same scent was present unmistakably when the body was brought in to the mortuary by the Golders Green men. Not only that but there was a certain stain upon the underclothes of the—er—'lady' which told me that she had most certainly handled and, indeed, carried the stolen prints about on her—him, I should say, of course. The inference was obvious—that the murder had been committed to get them."

"I see that I have been underrating your intelligence, Inspector," Hellner said quietly. "Go on."

"When, still later, I found those same stains upon the finger-tips of the murdered Mascagni, it wasn't difficult to put that two and two together and make four of them. I already knew that Mascagni was mixed up in the business, from the mere fact that he was one of the gentry in the car that tried to put paid to myself and Danny Regan as we were coming back from the mortuary. You must have had a very good suspicion even then, Baron, that you were extremely prominent in my mind in connection with the murder."

"For some reason not altogether explainable even to myself, I had," Hellner answered, those unmoving eyes of his still fixed upon the soft and extremely deceptive ones of the inspector. "Please go on; this is most interesting."

"You had another stroke of bad luck," McCarthy proceeded. "After you left Fasoli's last night, you very nearly crashed a taxi of a highly-esteemed friend of mine who, as a matter of fact, was turning into Soho to pick me up. As, apparently, you treated his protest with that contempt you seem to have for less fortunate persons of a humbler state than yourself, he turned and followed you, Baron."

"Followed me!"

"Followed you," McCarthy repeated. "As far as Grosvenor Square, and then again to this place."

"I saw nothing of him," the Baron snapped.

"He took remarkably good care of *that*," McCarthy informed him pleasantly. "As it happens he's by way of being an exceedingly shrewd chap who assists me no little from time to time, and he realized that he'd discovered the one join-up I'd been waiting for ever since a certain lady friend of yours had paid a call at Fasoli's in the afternoon."

"*Ach, Himmel!*" burst involuntarily from the German.

That change McCarthy had been waiting for came suddenly into the expression of those eyes. The revelation that he had been followed to Grosvenor Square and watched there, with the obvious implication that the visit connected him definitely with the Baroness Lena Eberhardt, had, unquestionably, been a shattering blow, both to his vanity and to his sense of security.

"Women," McCarthy said softly, "are the very divil in espionage, or any other kind of plotting for the matter of that. The dear things simply can't keep their teeth shut. Clever as they think they are, and cunning without a doubt, they almost invariably give the one lead away which sooner or later wrecks themselves and everyone concerned with them. My little friend, Tessa Domenico, will do just the same when they take her into the Yard for interrogation. I expect she will have been picked up by now. She'll squeal all she knows—you see if I'm not right, Hellner. And Fasoli—there's a poor kind of reed to lean upon when the going gets tough. The little birds warbling in the trees in Lincoln's Inn Fields can't get their notes out half as fast as Luigi Fasoli will spill all he knows."

A low, animal-like growl came from the throat of the German.

"Curse you," he began in little more than a hissed whisper. "Whatever happens, you, at least, will not be there to see it!"

"Get that idea out of your head entirely," McCarthy snapped, tensing himself. "I'll be there, right enough, and I'll give you one last piece of information, combined with prophecy, for luck. Heinrich will *not* take that stolen stuff out of England to-night!"

Like lightning one of his hands flashed downwards and outwards, cutting the pistol away from his mid-section; instantly it exploded and he heard the heavy bullet tear its way into the frame of the door. Simultaneously his right hand whizzed up into the man's face with terrific force, laying it open to the bone. The blood streamed from the wound, for a second blinding Hellner and giving McCarthy just that fraction of time he needed to get a grip upon the wrist of the German's gun hand.

But he was to find that in this man he had an opponent that it took more than one blow, terrible as it was, to stop.

Hellner's left fist crashed solidly into McCarthy's face, driving his head back against the door with almost stunning force. A moment later a knee in the groin gave him agonizing pain, but it also did something else upon which the other had certainly never counted.

It set the fighting Irish blood of the inspector ablaze with fury! Still gripping the man's gun-wrist, he lashed away at the bloodstained face with a viciousness which no man could have withstood for long. Hellner, as tall as McCarthy and every whit as powerful, dashed an iron-hard head into his face with shattering force—to be met the second time he tried it with an uppercut which nearly tore it from his shoulders. By sheer strength, McCarthy rushed his opponent back out of the door-way across the passage and up against the wall.

With the German trying to get a grip upon his throat, McCarthy dug him under the heart with that iron hand of his until the man's breathing became a short hard gasp which told its own story. But, although hurt, he was as deadly as a rattle-snake every second of the time.

But the blood he was losing was weakening him. It was pouring from his face in a torrent now, covering his own clothes, and McCarthy's, with the sticky fluid. In vain he tried to get a leg-lock and throw the Scotland Yard man, but only towards his own undoing, for McCarthy, expert at ju-jitsu as he was, nearly tore the limb from its socket.

Desperately he struggled to get the gun-hand free, but the inspector, realizing that if that happened his last moment had come, held on with the tenacity of a bull-dog. Again and again he lashed those wicked blows under the heart, but if they were slowing the man, he certainly was showing no sign of it beyond his gasping breath.

Then, with a sudden quick twist of his whole body, but still keeping his grip upon the wrist, McCarthy stooped quickly, whipped the man bodily to his shoulder, and sent him flying out, full length upon the floor. With the wrist held, the arm joint was wrenched completely out of its socket and the gun fell from limp, nerveless fingers.

But even then the other was not yet finished. One bloody hand shot out and gripped McCarthy by the ankle, and he endeavoured to pull the detective down upon the floor with him. And then it was that the Scotland Yard man got the hold he wanted.

Again stooping quickly, he got the cross-hold scissors grip upon the man's collar, drove his thumbs up under his ears, and pressed firmly. With a gasping sigh Hellner went limp all over, out to the wide, wide world!

Through every one of the German's pockets McCarthy went, searching him right down to his skin, but not a sign of the stolen dispositions could he find. Hellner must have passed them over to the Baroness Eberhardt during his hasty visit last night. At any rate that was the conclusion McCarthy came to, and devoutly hoped was the right one, since he was not carrying them upon him.

Pulling the unconscious man's hands behind him McCarthy started to look about him for something with which to secure him beyond any possible chance of freeing himself again. He found it in a strong silken coverlet which he ripped down and twisted into rope. Securely lashing Hellner's wrists together behind him, he then bound his ankles so that it was impossible to move an inch even if he managed to get up onto his feet. To make sure of that he lifted him, tossed him bodily upon one of the beds, ripped up a coverlet from another room and fastened him securely to it; in his unconscious state he did not dare to gag him in case the man choked to death. He was quite certain that with all the doors closed no one would ever hear him if he yelled his head off—these particular flats were not put up with breeze walls.

Hurrying through to the drawing-room he dialled the Yard and got through to Haynes just as that gentleman was leaving, presumably to keep his afternoon assignment.

"Bill," he said quickly, "put out a drag for Tessa Domenico right away. She's in the West End somewhere, probably shopping. Whatever happens she must not be allowed to get back here."

"Where's here?" Haynes asked pertinently.

Giving him the address, he further instructed that two men had better be put on assignment at the front entrance, in case the drag missed her.

"Now give orders to raid Fasoli's and pick Luigi up without further loss of time. Also every man known to belong to Mascagni's gang. Hold them for interrogation until I can get to the Yard."

"Have you got those stolen papers yet?" the A.C. questioned avidly.

"I shall have by evening, Bill," McCarthy informed him. "Don't let the thought of them trouble your mind. You keep that afternoon tea appointment."

"Are you still set on that crazy idea, Mac?" Haynes asked troubledly.

"More than ever," the inspector told him flatly. "Don't you let me down on that, whatever you do."

Ringing off before the Assistant Commissioner could raise any further objections, McCarthy hurried downstairs, pausing only for a moment at Delaney's box.

"I'm keeping the key of that flat for a little while," he informed that worthy who stared at his dishevelled and blood-stained condition in astonishment. "No one's to go near it. If they do you'll have trouble."

Out to Withers' taxi he hurried and to say that the burly William's astonishment at his plight was great is to considerably under-state his feelings.

"Blimey!" he ejaculated. "You ain't 'alf struck it rich, guv'nor. 'Ow many of 'em set abaht you?"

"Only one," McCarthy informed him, endeavouring to smile through a pair of split lips, "but he was plenty. Run me back to Dean Street to clean up and change my clothes."

"That suit's kind of bitched up proper, ain't it?" Withers observed commiseratingly.

"'Bitched' is no word for it," McCarthy said with a mournful shake of his head. "Savile Row stuff, Withers—and not yet paid for!"

Chapter XXII

A Two-Handed Raid!

It was exactly five o'clock when the inspector, still in "Big Bill's" taxi, arrived at Grosvenor Square—that hour when all those who have the time, or the inclination, generally partake of that cup which, we are told, cheers, but does not inebriate.

Although he had given himself very considerable attention after changing his ruined garments in Dean Street, there was still no shortage of marks upon his features, left there by the fists of the German secret-service agent. The well-nigh ruined Savile Row suit had been replaced by a different one entirely; one which any working man might have worn about his job.

The thing which was exercising McCarthy's mind most at the moment was the tricky job of getting into the Baroness Eberhardt's house without any of its occupants being any the wiser. To have gone up to the front door and demanded admission would have perhaps given that lady the very little time necessary to get that packet out of her hands, and even the house; after which the picking it up again would be the divil's own job, if ever it was accomplished at all.

As matters stood, with everything ready to smuggle those all-important plans out of the country that night, it was more than likely that not only the lady herself, but such of her household as were engaged upon this work of espionage would be well upon the *qui vive*, suspicious and on the look-out for anything that might be inimical to their plans. With the murders which had been committed in the process of acquiring the dispositions, they might well be on the watch for anything, or anyone, who might throw a monkey-wrench into their scheme, even at the last moment.

He had left Withers with the car around a corner of the square out of sight of the house, and was taking a quiet look over its exterior when his eyes fell upon the figure of Sir William Haynes approaching rapidly from the direction of Park Lane, and certainly the Assistant Commissioner had turned out in full regalia for the job. His morning coat was the very last word in fashion, his trousers were creased to a razor-like edge, while his shoes and top hat positively glittered. McCarthy promptly turned his back upon this spectacle of sartorial splendour—he had not the slightest wish for the A.C. to recognize him at that state of the game—but even before he did so, he saw that the face of his friend was wearing an anything but happy look. The A.C. was finding no particular pleasure in this portion of the business.

A second glance back showed him Sir William upon the top step outside the massive front entrance, and waiting, card in hand, to be admitted. The same glance also showed him that two heavy motor lorries which had come into the square had pulled up before a manhole in the pavement and which obviously belonged to the house; apparently the lady's winter supply of coal was about to be shot from them. Which gave the nimble-witted McCarthy an idea.

Hurrying back to the taxi he beckoned Withers out.

"Go and get hold of the boss of that gang of coalies and bring him here," he instructed. "The sight of them has shown me just how we're going to get into that house and be right on top of the people I want before they can get the slightest chance to slip what I'm after out of the way."

"Are we a-goin' to raid that there place, guv'nor? Jes' you an' me?"

"That's the idea as I see it at present, Withers," the inspector informed him. "With the aid of those worthy gentlemen we'll be on their necks almost before they know we've landed. And I don't doubt," he added, "that we'll get quite a bit of pleasurable excitement out of it."

Mr. Withers took one look at a suspicious-looking bulge under the left-hand side of the inspector's coat; a bulge which mutely intimated to him that McCarthy was carrying an automatic pistol, or revolver of fairly heavy calibre. Without a word he reopened the door by the driver's seat, stooped and dipped his hand down into his toolbox and took from it a weighty eighteen-inch spanner which he dropped into the pocket of his driving coat. It might not be needed, but with the inspector on this sort of a job you never knew what was going to happen next!

The burly person in charge of the coal gang having been brought before him by Withers, the inspector first showed him his warrant card, and then requested his aid—for a consideration. The gentleman in question promptly announced that he was only too proud and happy to be of service. Moreover, if the inspector thought there was likely to be a bit of a rough and tumble on hand, he and his mates would be only too happy to join in.

"The thing I most want to know," McCarthy said, after suitably thanking him for this sporting offer, "is what is your usual method in this business."

He was promptly enlightened as to the rites governing this procedure. When the cargo of the two motor-lorries, each carrying five tons of coal in sacks, had been shot down the manhole, two of his men went down the area steps to the basement and were admitted to the coal cellar. There they shovelled it off all nice and level for the servants of the house to get at. That had been the regular routine for the last three years, after which they were presented with a bottle of beer each and a tip, and then departed.

"Very well, then," McCarthy said. "When it comes to this going downstairs business, I and my friend, here, will make the descent and do the shovelling in the place of your men. So that by no chance any suspicion can possibly be aroused, two of your squad can slip around and sit in the taxi here until we get back, or at any rate keep out of sight until such time as it's propitious for them to reappear."

But Coalie Number One shook his head dubiously at this suggestion.

"It wouldn't work, guv'nor," he said, "because it's a tricky game an' somebody's got to know 'ow t' set abaht it. We're watched all the time by that there bulldoggin' butler, name of Heinrich, or some such, 'oo looks t' me like as if 'e's been one o' them there sergeants in the Jerry army we used to run up again in the war. 'E foxes y' all the time as if you was goin' t' pinch somethink. I'll go dahn wiv yer, then 'e can't think as there's nothink wrong, because 'e knows me well, though 'e ain't none the more pleasant for that. Arf a mo'!"

He slipped round the corner to the motor-trucks and presently reappeared with two of his men who promptly divested themselves of their leather aprons, sleeved waist-coats and headgear, and handed them over to Withers and McCarthy.

"Nah, you two stick 'ere in this keb," the foreman ordered, "and don't git aht of it till you're told. Unless," he added, "you 'ear a proper bull an' a cow goin' on, then come dahn and do sunnink useful towards it."

Assured fervently upon this point, McCarthy and the monumental Withers followed their leader to the lorries. When the time arrived, he led the way down the area steps to a small but extremely solid door upon which he knocked; McCarthy noted that three heavy bolts were drawn before it was opened. Evidently the house of the Baroness Eberhardt was one which invited no intruders below stairs.

McCarthy decided that the coalie had not been far out in his appraisement of the tremendously thick-set and lowering-faced man who opened the door to them. If he had not been a German non-commissioned officer of the old, vicious type, then he, McCarthy, was a very mistaken man. He gave them no "Good day" or anything else civil, but merely pointed along a dark and dungeon-like passage towards one of three doors which stood in a row. Two, the inspector saw, were heavily barred and padlocked upon the outside. The one pointed to was open and was evidently the huge cellar which could take ten tons of coal at a time.

Straight for it their leader went and, with a gruff: "Nah, then, set abaht it!" led the way into the most gloomy-looking cavern McCarthy remembered to have ever seen in his life. It was lit only by the ray of daylight from the manhole in the pavement. At the word of command they crashed realistically into the enormous bank of coal, which was still being further enlarged by the men on top. Hovering about the door the whole of the time was this butler, Heinrich, who looked as much like a bulldog about to spring as anything else.

"'Ow abaht it if 'e don't make a shift, guv'nor?" "Big Bill" muttered through shut teeth.

"Then he'll have to be shifted!" McCarthy answered in the same way.

But five minutes passed and there was still no sign of the welcome happening, and McCarthy had just made up his mind to act for himself in the matter when from above a bell rang peremptorily, three times. Muttering to himself in German, though in too low a tone for the inspector to pick up his words, the man, after another keen glance at the three of them, moved towards the bottom of a stone staircase some twenty feet further along the passage.

It was difficult to hear the man's footsteps on the stairs above the noise of the rasping of the shovels and the sliding of the coal, but McCarthy gave him what he considered time enough to reach the first landing and get out of sight, then quickly slipped into the passage. The attempt would have to be made now.

It was only reasonable to believe that the baroness herself would be engaged with Haynes, and possibly other guests, though he doubted much that with what was afoot in her household upon this particular day she would have invited any callers. Whispering to the coalie that he was about to make the effort he had spoken of, and calling to Withers to follow him, he crept cautiously for the bottom of the staircase.

He had scarcely started when they heard the sound of the man returning, his feet making a clear ring upon the stone steps as he descended. Something had aroused his suspicion, though what McCarthy could not for the life of him think. Then it suddenly occurred to him that the perfectly clean faces of Withers and himself, entirely free from coal-dust or any other earmarks of their supposed occupation, must in itself have been suspicious to a man of this type.

The features of their friend shovelling away in the cellar were as black as the medium he worked with; so also were those of the men upstairs shooting the stuff down, while those of Withers, although at no time to be taken as a specimen of a well-groomed man, were as white as the driven snow in comparison. As for his own face, he was perfectly well aware that after his recent ablutions and despite the bruises he exhibited, it must fairly shine like that of a well-scrubbed infant. It had been a damned foolish oversight, and was no doubt the cause of this suspicious-natured man determining not to leave them for a moment. Well, it was too late to do anything about it now, and upstairs they had to get by hook or crook.

The instant the man set foot in the passage again his hard little eyes fell upon McCarthy crouching there, a good five yards or more from the cellar in which he should have been at work.

"*Ach! Himmel!*" he snarled, and turned with the obvious intention of shouting a warning to someone he must have known to have been within hearing up the stairs. That was as far as he got!

Like a tiger McCarthy flung himself at him and any sound that might have come from his mouth was stopped by a crashing smash which split it to the gums. It was followed by a second which landed upon the man's jaw and sent his head back with a jerk. The blow was one which would have dropped most men, but this bull-like creature shook it off and put his hand to his mouth to shout to those upstairs. Then, and before McCarthy could make another move to stop the dread sound, something cracked down upon the man's skull which dropped him like a stone. It was Withers' spanner.

"Beg parding, sir," that worthy said, "but I knows you ain't got time to waste on the likes of 'im, and if 'e'd a-started 'ollerin', nobody knows 'oo 'e's a-goin' t' bring down. Wot do we do wiv 'im?"

"Put him into one of these cellars," McCarthy whispered. "They'll hear nothing from him here."

An order no sooner given than carried out.

Instantly the inspector crept to the bottom of the stairs, listened for a second, then began to make his way up them. He was nearly to the top when he discovered that Withers was on his heels.

"I don't know about you, Withers," he whispered dubiously. "I can't tell how strong the gang here is, and I don't know that I've any right to risk you stopping a bullet or something equally pretty. After all you're a civilian."

"You can call me a bleedin' copper for the time being," Mr. Withers gave back. "A sort of a 'special' like."

"Somewhere on this landing we're going to run into a nest of servants," the inspector continued. "A house of this size is bound to be pretty well staffed, and you can bet on all of them, men and women alike, belonging to the same breed. Once they realize what we are they'll turn nasty."

"So much the worse f'r them," "Big Bill" said stolidly. "What's the move, guv'nor?"

McCarthy pointed ahead to a door on the landing, from behind which they could hear the murmur of voices.

"That I fancy will be the kitchen," he whispered. "And with Heinrich out of the way, if we can only manage to fasten them up there, we'll have a clear field ahead of us upstairs."

Withers nodded towards the key plainly to be seen in the lock.

"What's the matter with turning that on 'em, and there they are, so t' speak."

McCarthy shook his head. "It's a bit too easy to be true, Withers," he returned. "We don't know what other doors there may be leading out of that room that they can escape by, and perhaps land us in a trap. We've got to get in first, and make sure of that."

From his shoulder-holster he drew his automatic pistol, then from his coat pocket took its silencer, and jammed it down tight on the barrel.

"We want no noise to give any warning above," he explained. "The quicker and quieter this job is done, the better."

Without hesitation he walked to the door, opened it, and passed through, followed by Withers, his spanner ready for any emergencies. That luck was with them to the extent that the majority, at least, of the servants of the house seemed to be congregated there was very apparent, and equally so the fact that they were completely taken by surprise at this most unexpected arrival.

The principal one seemed to be an enormously fat *chef*, garbed in the recognized uniform of his profession, and whose face went deadly pale as his eyes fell upon the weapon which McCarthy waved in an arc which covered the whole of the gathering.

At a large kitchen table were seated four maids, and a couple of menservants; all, without exception, were definitely Teutonic in the cast of their features. One of the latter made to rise to his feet, but sat down again as McCarthy turned the barrel of his ugly-looking weapon upon him.

"I think you'd better remain seated," the inspector advised grimly. "I should be very sorry to have to perforate anyone here with this gun of mine, but I can assure you that I will without the slightest hesitation if there's any attempt at resistance from any one of you." The barrel moved round to cover the *chef* again. "I think," he went on pleasantly, "that you'd better be seated as well, Herr *Chef*—and over in that corner there where there aren't any drawers handy, likely to contain cutlery. You'll quite understand that you're under arrest, though how far you're guilty of anything against the peace of this realm will be gone into later."

His eyes went slowly about the room taking in another two doors, one of which opened, he saw, into a large pantry. Crossing to it he found that it was illuminated and ventilated by a very small window, the outer side of which was covered

with perforated zinc, and was certainly not one to be nego-
tiated by any there who were all definitely of thick, not to
say stodgy, build. Not even the slimmest of the maids could
have been assisted through it, and as for the *chef*, himself,
he would be as safe in there as behind bars.

"I'll trouble you all, ladies included, to lift your hands
in the direction of the ceiling, and keep them there—otherwise…Withers," he continued when the order had been
promptly obeyed, "just go round and pass your hands over
the gentlemen's clothes for any concealed weapons they may
have about them. They probably haven't any, but on the other
hand they may have. I don't think you need trouble about
the ladies. They don't seem to be the sort that would carry
arms, or use them with any skill if they did."

Mr. Withers having searched all the males so assiduously
that the probability of their having anything lethal upon
them was very remote, McCarthy indicated the door of the
pantry with his pistol.

"The gentlemen first," he invited, "and keeping their
hands well above their heads. By the way," he addressed
himself to the *chef*, who despite the almost waxen pallor of
his face was sweating profusely. "How many more are there
in the servants' hall—if that's the correct term?"

He was told that with the exception of the *major-domo*, one
Heinrich Buchel, the servants of the house were all present.

"Splendid!" McCarthy exclaimed, in very genuine satisfaction. "And perhaps you can also inform me what guests
are upstairs—with the exception of one that I happen to
know of."

He was informed by one of the maids that the baroness
was entertaining but one person at that moment, though
they understood that she had others coming later to dinner.

"I fear they are in for a lean time," the inspector said
with a sad shake of his head. "Now step in, please, and make

yourselves as comfortable as may be. And understand this," he warned, "that there'll be a man on guard who will have no hesitation at all about making himself extremely unpleasant to anyone who attempts to break out. No hesitation *whatever*," he emphasized.

Closing the door, he carefully locked it, then proceeded to prop a chair beneath its handle. "I think we'll have our friend the coalie upstairs just as a precaution," he said. "If that professor of cookery chose to hurl his weight against the door I doubt either lock or chair would hold."

"He's scared stiff; he won't try no bustin' aht. When I run me 'ands over 'im he was shakin' like a jelly."

"We'll take no chances," McCarthy said, and, calling up the gentleman in question, proceeded to give him his instructions. As the gentleman, anticipating some such job, had brought his shovel with him, this latter article was considered quite sufficient weapon for the business in hand. As he assured McCarthy he would have no hesitation whatever in using it upon anyone of Germanic breed, male or female, having done two years in a German prison camp, he was left to the assignment with full confidence that his end of it would not go far wrong.

"And now, Withers, although not garbed for such an occasion, in fact, very much otherwise, we'll depart upstairs to the drawing-room, and pay our compliments to the baroness. I doubt she'll be pleased to see us, but we can't help that."

"I'll bet as Sir William gets a surprise when we blow in," "Big Bill" prophesied with a cavernous grin.

"I'll bet he does," McCarthy agreed. "In fact the certainty that he would is one of the biggest things I had in mind in getting him here. 'Twill teach him that even Assistant Commissioners don't know as much as they think they do."

Chapter XXIII

The Inspector Clears Things Up!

The baroness, in Sir William Haynes' opinion, was at her very best that afternoon. Never, upon the several occasions that the Assistant Commissioner had the pleasure of being entertained by her in her own house, had she ever appeared so radiantly beautiful, so generally charming as upon that day. Whatever surprise may have filled her when the totally unexpected visit was announced, no sign of it or, indeed, perturbation of any kind, was permitted to show upon her features.

Just what the devil McCarthy was playing at in insisting upon his taking her by surprise in the manner that he had was more than Sir William could make out, but he was quite certain that that engaging officer would find himself very badly in the cart before he was finished if he attempted to involve this particular lady in the robbery in Whitehall. For his own part, he kept things professional sedulously out of the conversation, and explained his visit by the fact that he had had a duty call to make at another house in Grosvenor Square, and had availed himself of the opportunity. Nor did he even mention the name of Detective Inspector McCarthy, though more than once the baroness gave him very definite leads in that direction. Unquestionably the debonair inspector was a source of considerable interest to her.

But he noticed that, whilst the perfect hostess in every possible way, the lady was inclined to be somewhat restless, and moved about the room a good deal. In particular did she keep moving towards the huge bay windows of her drawing-room which opened out upon a marble and tessellated balcony overlooking the square and immediately overhanging a small, admirably-designed rock garden.

Despite the fact that the lady was graciousness herself, Sir William, in the circumstances, was beginning to find it difficult to make conversation against time—and how long McCarthy expected him to go on with this damned senseless tomfoolery he had no more idea than the dead. He had, as requested, given considerable attention to the lady's butler, or *major-domo*, whichever she preferred to call him, when that certainly saturnine-looking person had served the afternoon tea. He most certainly had been entirely typical of the German under-officer, and one thing was very certain: that despite the perfection of his manner as a servant his appearance, with his heavy, brutish features, was far from prepossessing.

But, Sir William argued to himself even as he chatted gaily to the lady, that did not make his mistress party to a gigantic scheme of espionage. Plenty of thoroughly worthy people were ill-favoured, and it was no part of the English system of justice to judge a man by his looks alone. Had it been there were quite a number of eminently respectable officers at Scotland Yard itself who would have been sojourning upon the "Moor."

And yet, as he watched the wonderfully gowned figure of his hostess moving gracefully about her drawing-room, there was an uneasiness in the mind of Sir William. McCarthy was not the man to make horrible bloomers of the kind which involved persons of social, and financial consequence, where a mistake would have landed the administration of the Yard, and himself in particular, in the devil of a mess if things did not pan out the right way.

Recalling to mind the extraordinary speed with which the indefatigable inspector had joined up the robbery at Whitehall with the murder in Soho Square, and also, later, that of Mascagni as well as that of the old coffee-stall man, nothing he could do managed to shake the doubt which insisted upon lingering in his mind. It seemed incredible that there should be the slightest connection between this lady and those ghastly happenings, and he could only hope that when McCarthy got down to rock bottom he would find that he had been following a false trail where she was concerned. In any case he meant giving the inspector but another five minutes' grace and then taking his leave of Grosvenor Square, and herself, for the time being.

But no more than two of those minutes had passed when he received what was very possibly the greatest shock of his professional career, for the folding doors of the drawing-room were suddenly flung open, and instead of the saturnine-looking Heinrich appearing to announce other guests, there upon the threshold stood McCarthy himself, while at the back of him towered the enormous figure of "Big Bill" Withers, his spanner clenched in his massive right fist.

And that McCarthy had been through a strenuous time since he had last set eyes upon him was only too palpable. Upon his face were marks of battle but recently inflicted, and which certainly would not be removed in a hurry. Additionally the ancient suit he was wearing appeared to be grimed with coal dust although his much bruised face was fairly clear of that substance. But what troubled Haynes most, when he had got over the shock of this un-heralded appearance, was the look of quiet triumph which shone in the inspector's soft, Italian-looking eyes; a look which he had seen too often to make any mistake about it. Whatever his appearance there and in that garb and condition might portend, there was no doubt in the mind of the Assistant Commissioner that, to use that pregnant American term, McCarthy had brought home the bacon once again.

For perhaps five seconds there was dead silence in the room, other than that ejaculation which had been forced from Haynes at the appearance of this strangely assorted pair. It was broken first by the Baroness Eberhardt, who had stood staring at this very different McCarthy from the one she had met at Verrey's as she might have done at some apparition from the grave.

"This is a totally unexpected pleasure, Inspector," she said without a sign of perturbation, but McCarthy noticed that the smile which came to her lips was fixed and rigid, and somehow gave a very different expression to her face.

"Well, now," he said smoothly, "I don't doubt but that it would be. In the circumstances I'd probably be surprised myself. But, somehow or other I had the feeling when I left you at Verrey's that it wouldn't be long before we met again."

"Most interesting." Then she turned to Sir William. "Had you any idea that Inspector McCarthy proposed to pay me this—er—unorthodox call?"

Sir William Haynes started, then glared at the cause of his discomfiture. "Not the slightest," he answered quickly. "Though, in a way," he amended quickly, "I sort of had an idea that he—er—would be somewhere in—in this vicinity."

The baroness nodded. "I see," she said thoughtfully. "Would it be asking official secrets to tell me the reason for this visit, Inspector? There is some motive behind your call, I feel sure."

"Well, in a sense 'tis the result of following up a 'hunch' of mine to begin with. I don't know whether the word is familiar to you, Baroness, it's an American one and means doing a thing without the slightest rhyme, reason, or anything else at the bottom of it all: I do that sort of thing, as Sir William here can tell you, and an infernal nuisance I generally make of myself while I'm at it. 'Twas just such a 'hunch' that made me have your friend Baron Hellner—I believe that's the name—followed out of Soho Square after the murder of the so-called Madame Rohner."

"Ah, the Soho Square murder," she returned lightly. "But first I should correct you upon one point. I have no friend of that name."

"It's probably not the right one," McCarthy said smoothly. "But 'twill do for the time being. As for his not being a friend of yours then I admit that I am under a misapprehension. I got the idea through his calling here last night, after the murder of Mascagni."

"Mascagni," she murmured.

"Exactly, Floriello Mascagni. The man whose gang, at Hellner's instigation, killed an inoffensive old man called Anselmi to get hold of his coffee-stall as a medium for getting the body of the *pseudo* Madame Rohner out of Soho Square."

"Madame Rohner," she murmured in the same vague way.

McCarthy nodded. "Quite so," he said. "And that was the second reason that brought me here to-day. If you hadn't mentioned the fact at Verrey's that you had that morning been to consult your especial medium, clairvoyant, or whatever the right term is, and moreover informed Sir William and me that you had made the appointment by telephone, I should probably never have given you a second thought—in connection with the murder and the theft of those dispositions from Whitehall, of course."

From him the baroness looked inquiringly at Haynes, who stared vacantly at the ceiling wondering what the devil was coming next, then back again at McCarthy. Her face was a perfect study in complete blankness.

"I'm afraid," she began, when McCarthy with a wave of his hand interrupted her.

"We'll come to that later. It will be sufficient for me to mention that I happen to know that the stolen papers were handed to you last night by the Baron Hellner and he was assured that Heinrich would have them out of England to-day."

"Assured by whom, Inspector?" she inquired.

"By yourself, Baroness," he informed her. "Your memory is surely not so poor that you've forgotten that. He brought them to you immediately he had received them at a dirty little wine shop in Soho, known as the *Circolo Venezia*, kept by one Fasoli—a place, by the way, with which you're quite familiar, as you undoubtedly called there yesterday afternoon. It was after Hellner had left that place that our unpleasant little friend, Ludwig, murdered Mascagni, also at Hellner's instigation. Unfortunately," the inspector went on with his ingratiating smile, "his unfortunate lack of manners towards those he considers to be his inferiors in life, aroused the ire of a certain friend of mine, who followed him to Grosvenor Square, and, with great perspicacity, listened in upon the conversation you held with Hellner at your own door. A great mistake that, Baroness; it's amazing how voices carry in the stillness of the black-out."

The lady addressed said nothing; her smile was just as set as it had always been, but McCarthy saw her eyes wander towards the rope of an old-fashioned bell-pull set beside one of the bay windows opening down on to the square. Lazily he moved to place himself between her and it.

"It would do no good whatever, Baroness, to call either for assistance or—or whatever else it might be in your mind to do. The whole of your staff of servants are bottled up where they won't get out in a hurry, with an extremely capable gentleman standing guard over them with a shovel. Heinrich is in equally bad shape, and certainly not in a position to answer any call upon him that you might make."

"Heinrich is a captive?" she exclaimed sharply.

"Well—er—scarcely that, though quite as good. I had the pleasure, the extreme pleasure I might say, of knocking that gentleman stone cold before making my appearance up here. Or rather," he corrected hastily, "my friend, Mr. Withers here, performed that very valuable contribution to this raid, and what he does in that line, he does very thoroughly, I can assure you."

"Where is Baron Hellner now?" she demanded sharply.

"That particular gentleman, who, by the way, you don't know, is at the present moment reposing in a cell at either Vine Street or Cannon Row police station, if everything's gone according to my instructions, which I don't doubt that it has. With him, or nearby, is that extremely beautiful, though I regret to say unlucky young lady, the Signorina Tessa Domenico, by whose aid Mascagni was put on the spot for his murder. By this time every soul concerned with that crime, and the Soho Square murder, is under arrest, with two notable exceptions, Ludwig and yourself. That will be rectified within the very near future."

As he spoke he glanced through the window to see slowly coming into the square the car which had driven Tessa Domenico and her belongings from Doughty Street to Park Lane. At the wheel, perched up in his usual jack-in-the-box fashion, was the dwarf, Ludwig.

"Withers," he said quietly, "if you go down to the basement you'll probably run into the very one I was just speaking about. The dwarf we saw drive Tessa Domenico to Park Lane this morning. Make no bones whatever about him, and be sure to intercept him before he can get up to the kitchen where we have the others. I shouldn't like to find our stalwart friend the coalie dead with a knife through his back, which would most probably be his finish if that gargoyle-faced merchant gets wind at what he's at."

"Leave that to me, guv'nor," "Big Bill" said grimly, and departed swiftly out and down the stairs. At once McCarthy faced the baroness, all sign of lightness gone from him.

"I'll have those stolen papers, Baroness Eberhardt," he said grimly. "To deny any knowledge of them is simply futile. They were placed in your hands last night to smuggle out of England by the medium of your servant, Heinrich. In any case it is my duty to inform you that you are under arrest upon a charge of espionage, and, further, of complicity in, and accessory before and after, the fact of three murders. It is also my duty to inform you that anything you may have to say will be taken down and used in evidence against you."

Just who was to do the "taking down" was rather more than McCarthy could have said at the moment, unless, of course, it was Sir William Haynes. That gentleman sat staring from one to the other of them as though his mind was in a perfect maze, and made no movement whatever to suggest that he was about to become McCarthy's amanuensis in this paralysing business.

Without a word, but with a dejected shrug of her shoulders which seemed to acknowledge defeat, the baroness moved slowly towards an inlaid *buhl* table which stood just inside the door. Laying a hand upon the handle of one of its drawers she drew it open. But a certain sudden rigidity in the set of her back and her shoulders warned McCarthy that this woman was not yet defeated. With a sharp exclamation which brought Haynes to his feet, he dashed across the room at her and seized her wrist as she half turned, in her hand an automatic pistol! Swift as he was, she had even then time to open the safety catch and the bullet which most certainly would have found a billet in one or other of them ploughed through the ceiling of the drawing-room. Nor was it an easy matter to disarm her, for she fought like a wild cat and he was to find that that litheness of movement of hers was a matter of sinew, and not acquired grace. It took a full minute of hard struggle, in which he was aided by a still semi-dazed Sir William, before he forced her down into an armchair and handcuffed her by one wrist to it. Even then she left some fresh marks upon his already maltreated features.

"There's nothing for it, Bill, but to have a squad here and go through this place from the cellars to the attic. Those papers are here right enough, you can be sure of that."

At which moment Withers appeared, lugging up the stairs with his feet trailing against every tread, the inanimate form of the dwarf, Ludwig.

"I 'ad to land 'im one, sir," he half-apologized. "'E may be short in the 'eight, so t' speak, but blimey 'e's as strong as a gorilla fr'm the waist up."

"Tie him up, Withers, and make dead sure of him," McCarthy ordered. "He's due to swing for the murder of Flo. Mascagni."

A shout went up from the street. Running to the window McCarthy saw the thick-set form of Heinrich stealing across the square as rapidly as it was possible for him to move without drawing too much attention to himself. In a flash it crossed the inspector's mind that he was the person who had those papers in his possession! He was all ready to get away when Ludwig called for him with the car, as had no doubt been previously arranged. The baroness knew it and had she been able to have got that gun unmolested she would have held them up there until her servant got clear away. Heinrich had seen his opportunity for escape while the coalie was upstairs in that kitchen; had probably heard Withers' scuffle with the dwarf and realized that it was now or never, if he was to fulfil his mission.

With a cry McCarthy flung open one of the long windows opening to the balcony, crossed it and without hesitation vaulted the parapet and landed in the garden with an anything but pleasant thud. For a moment it shook the wind out of him, but in the next he was over the fence and streaking across the square after the German as fast as ever a fox ran before hounds. He was nearly up with him at the corner of Grosvenor Street when the man suddenly turned and pulled a gun from his pocket. Without hesitation McCarthy charged blindly in at him, and a shot which would have most likely ended his mortal career whined past his ear as he came to grips with the man. As it was he took a wicked rap on the side of the head with the heavy weapon which, for a moment, sent him dizzy.

But by sheer main strength and the force of his attack he rushed the man back against the railings of a house as he thought; it proved to be the gate leading down to the area which flew open and the pair of them dived headlong down the stone steps. Twice the German's head contacted heavily as they rolled over each other in their descent—and once McCarthy's hit the side of the wall with force enough to send him sick and dizzy, but he clung on like a bull-terrier, although after the strenuous efforts of that day he began to find his strength waning.

But, as it happened, help was close at hand for the pair of coalies who had been left in Withers' taxi had been observers of all that had taken place and were making their way to the spot at which the pair had disappeared as hard as their legs could carry them.

By this time Heinrich and the inspector were engaged in a slogging bout in which no rules were observed by either, and the German was using his feet as well as his hands to escape the fate he knew was certain to follow capture. Another couple of minutes would have seen that end well in sight, for McCarthy, though sticking to the much heavier man like a leech, was reeling in front of him like a man "out" upon his feet.

He had just taken a heavy kick which had nearly knocked what little breath he had out of him when the first of the coalies took the steps at a dive and, believing in the sound principle of an eye for an eye where a fight was concerned put his heavy number ten boot into the German's stomach with such accuracy and force that the man doubled up like a jack knife. In the next moment the second was upon him and the pair bore him to the ground and kept him there while McCarthy searched his pockets. In a concealed one, stitched underneath the man's shirt, he found the oilskin-covered packet which meant so much.

The trio were forcing the German up the steps again when a constable came round the corner almost on top of them. He was a young man but newly sent in from the country, and he stared at this curiously assorted quartette as though he could scarcely believe his eyes. In the brief time that he had known Grosvenor Square he certainly had never struck anything like this particular lot before.

"Give me your cuffs," the most battered looking of the lot said in a tone of authority, and holding out his hand for those highly desirable articles.

"Not so fast; not so fast," the C. Division rookie returned with a calm wave of his hand and speaking in a strong Wiltshire accent. "We'll hear some more about this before I give anybody anything. This looks to me like a case of Common Assault."

"It'll be the most uncommon one you've ever heard of if you don't dig out those cuffs when you're ordered," the inspector snapped at him, his hand still held out for the articles requested.

Doubt assailed the gentleman from the country. There was something in the tone of this battered-looking object that seemed to imply authority; a man, this, who sounded as though he was used to being obeyed when he gave orders.

"Who might you be?" C. 1674 inquired, the doubt he was feeling strong in his voice.

"Well," McCarthy answered, through bruised lips, "I might be anybody, I might even be the Prime Minister or, come to that, His Holiness the Pope in disguise. I could even be one of the reigning monarchs travelling *incognito*. But as it happens I'm not. My name's McCarthy, and I'm an inspector of the C.I.D. Do you want to see my Warrant Card?"

"No, sir," he was hurriedly answered, and the cuffs produced and snapped upon the German's wrists in the twinkling of an eye.

McCarthy looked at his fellow guardian of the peace, a whimsical twist at the side of his mouth.

"And how do you know that I really *am* Inspector McCarthy?" he asked quietly. "You've handed over your cuffs without the slightest proof that I'm who I say. I've seen men run out of the Force for less."

"I—I took your word for it, sir," C. 1674 stammered, a look of perturbation growing rapidly upon his face.

"That's the way," McCarthy said. "That's the way, lad. Take everything that's told you in London for gospel! 'Tis the most truthful town in the world. Follow up that idea and you'll either be one of two things. You'll either be looking for a job, or they'll make you an inspector—and then the good Lord look after you for nobody else will."

To receive a free catalog of Poisoned Pen Press titles, please provide your name, address, and email address in one of the following ways:

Phone: 1-800-421-3976
Facsimile: 1-480-949-1707
Email: info@poisonedpenpress.com
Website: www.poisonedpenpress.com

Poisoned Pen Press
6962 E. First Ave. Ste 103
Scottsdale, AZ 85251